TO DARE
A SEAL

a Sin City SEALs novel

SARA JANE
STONE

Entangled Publishing, LLC
2614 South Timberline Road
Suite 109
Fort Collins, CO 80525
Visit our website at www.entangledpublishing.com.

Brazen is an imprint of Entangled Publishing, LLC. For more information on our titles, visit www.brazenbooks.com.

Edited by Heather Howland and Stephen Morgan
Cover design by Heather Howland
Cover art from iStock

Manufactured in the United States of America

First Edition November 2015

ENTANGLED
BRAZEN

For Heather, the editor extraordinaire who made this story shine!

Chapter One

Four flirtatious fools. Three tipsy blondes. Two drunken sailors. If she looked in the bar's back room, Natalie Lewis suspected she'd find a partridge in a pear tree roosting on the broken neon BOTTOM'S UP sign.

"Two more days until vacation," she murmured, scooping ice into a pint glass for Drunken Sailor Number One's water. If a road trip to Sin City to play the maid of honor role in her little sister's wedding was considered a vacation. Behind her, the front door to the bar swung open, and Natalie glanced over her shoulder.

She let out a low, frustrated growl. It was as if the universe had sensed that her Monday afternoon shift needed an extra something to drive her bat-shit crazy and sent her five brown-haired, blue-eyed men led by U.S. Navy SEAL Jack Barnes— Chief Barnes to his teammates. Jack stopped in front of her bar and flashed his signature hand-over-your-panties smile to Natalie.

Another woman might have obeyed, falling for the

SEAL's potent combination of muscle and charm. But she was more of a give-me-your-boxers kind of girl.

Natalie eyed the pack. "Join a new team, Jack?"

The leader of the group shook his head, locks of straight brown hair falling across his forehead. "Thankfully, no," he said, reaching up to brush the stray hair from his face. The sleeve of his T-shirt moved down his arm, revealing his toned, oh-so impressive bicep. Not that she was looking. When it came to Jack, she found it was best to just say no. No looking. No touching. No wanting what she couldn't have.

"Miss Natalie Lewis," the SEAL continued. "Meet my brothers—"

"Big brothers," the man behind Jack's right shoulder added, hooking his thumbs into his belt beside the metal buckle shaped like the state of Texas. The motion drew her attention to the man's protruding belly. "Just because you're a SEAL doesn't mean I can't still take you down, kid."

Not a chance.

She mentally labeled Brother Number One an arrogant blowhard.

"Colton," Jack said, pointing to Mr. Belt Buckle. "Andrew, Charles, and Patrick. Not that you need to remember their names. They're heading out tomorrow." Jack's smile faded as he gestured to the pack behind him. "Some of the guys from the team are on their way. Mind if we stake out the corner tables?"

"All yours," she said. "What can I get for you?"

"The usual for me," Jack said.

Speaking for the pack, Colton ordered four lite beers on draft, adding a wink to the end of his request. Natalie stared blankly at Mr. Belt Buckle. She never flirted with customers. An extra buck here or there in tips wasn't worth the aggravation of telling a sailor to take a hike at the end of the night if he got the wrong impression.

When it came to her love life, she called the shots. And she never followed the relationship path. That road led to a dead end labeled hurt and rejection. Bouncing between foster homes as a teenager, she'd had her fill of both, thank you very much.

She was done with people walking into her life, telling her how it was and how it would be, then abandoning her without any concern for the damage they'd left in their wake. The foster families, even the well-meaning ones, had seemingly stripped away her right to make decisions about her life. And then, when they'd found her wanting, they'd returned her to social services.

All of the foster families had said something similar when the social worker had come to pick up Natalie and her younger sister.

Not what we're looking for in a daughter.

Too rebellious.

Too stubborn.

Those overheard comments still stung, like a wound she'd managed to cover with a Band-Aid, but it refused to heal.

Of course, her foster parents always waited until she'd started to trust them before they got rid of her. They didn't send her packing until she'd finally let down her guard and hoped for some sort of permanence, for something good to happen to her and her sister. Then they took it all away, replacing her hope with hurt.

And after a handful of brief romantic flings, she'd learned that dating led to the same dead end. Even the well-meaning guys just wanted to control her "for her own good." If happily ever after did exist, it only happened to other people. Never to her.

So she steered clear of getting close to anyone besides her sister. And that relationship had work-in-progress stamped all over it.

She glanced again at Jack and his bulging biceps, and that smile… His too charming grin made her heart stop one moment and spurred her temper the next.

"I'll be back with your drinks." She turned and headed for the row of taps behind the bar.

"Feisty little thang," Mr. Belt Buckle announced in his thick Texas accent. His words carried over the flirtatious fools, tipsy blondes, and drunken sailors.

Natalie gritted her teeth and focused on pouring the blowhard's beer.

"Leave her alone, Colton," Jack said in the same no-nonsense tone he used when the youngest members of his SEAL team drank themselves under the table and started acting stupid.

"Don't tell me you're hitting that," Colton sneered, and the pack of brothers cackled. "Kid, you wouldn't know what to do with a wild one like her. There's no way you've upped your game that much since you joined the Navy."

Natalie set the glass down hard on the tray, sending beer spilling over the rim. *Wouldn't know what to do?* Every time Jack walked into her bar, her imagination rioted, parading images of exactly what Jack could do with her.

He pressed her up against a wall, those powerful arms caging her in.

His eyes locked on her as she unbuttoned his pants and reached inside. And then she wrapped her hand around him, demanding that he follow her lead.

Fantasy Jack would know exactly what to do. He'd keep his mouth shut, biting back the stupid pick-up lines he tossed across the bar. And he'd listen to her instructions.

If she let down her guard, she just might join the women who walked into Bottom's Up, took one look at Jack, and offered up their underwear. The man was a walking, talking Prince Charming. They all went home with him because they thought he was offering something more. But Natalie knew better than to fall for an illusion.

She shouldered the tray and headed for the corner table.

"Here you go, boys," she said as she passed out the drinks. Then she turned to go, but something held her back. Literally, a tug along her waist. She glanced over her shoulder and saw Colton's hand wrapped around her apron strings.

"Let go," she and Jack snapped simultaneously.

Chuckling, the Texas-sized jerk released her. "Tie my baby brother up in these strings? These days he might break free. Before he joined the damn Navy, we used to do the same thing, leaving him in a field until he missed the call for dinner. You wouldn't know it from looking at him, but he was a weakling growing up."

"Jack, a weakling?" She moved to the side of the Navy SEAL's wooden chair. Jack's fairy-tale charm presented a danger to her carefully ordered life, but she refused to let this blowhard stomp all over him.

Leaning over Jack, she smashed her number one rule to pieces beside the corner table and offered him a peek down her scoop-neck tank top. Her breasts were average, hovering in the middle ground between large and small. But Jack's eyes still widened, taking in the view before his gaze returned to her face.

She touched his bicep, running her fingers over his skin to the edge of his T-shirt. And he tensed beneath her hand. "He doesn't feel weak," she said, adding a sultry edge to her tone.

"You should have seen him when he was younger," Colton said. "Arms like twigs."

Mr. Belt Buckle's words acted like a propellant, and her whisper of anger turned into a wild fire. The flames leaped past control. Her gaze locked with Jack's blue eyes. Most nights, she was glad the bar stood between her and the Prince Charming of the Navy SEALs. But hearing Colton Barnes hurl insults—as if the eldest Barnes sibling had spent Jack's entire life looking for the right words to torment his little brother—something inside her snapped.

"I try to never look back on the past." She knew the words were a lie. The past followed her around, dictating every relationship in her life. But she pressed on, refusing to let Mr. Belt Buckle have the upper hand. "Not when the present is so enticing," she added.

Jack raised an eyebrow, silently posing the question: Are you serious?

You bet your fancy little trident pin I am.

Without a second thought, she ran her hand up his shoulder, not stopping until her fingers wove through his hair. She lowered her lips to his, maintaining a tight hold on his head. One quick kiss. One touch. Nothing more.

But oh holy hell, the feel of his mouth, the taste of his surprise, the moment when he parted his lips, offering to claim her—

She broke the kiss and stepped away. She took a deep breath, searching for Calm and Collected Natalie as she turned away from Jack.

Behind her, Colton and company whooped and demanded another kiss. But Natalie knew better. One kiss that left her feeling as though she'd hot-wired her dormant sexual needs was a stupid mistake. A second might fully awaken wants and needs that she flat-out refused to let Prince Charming fulfill.

She threw a smirk toward Jack and the boys, then turned and walked back to the bar. Work. She needed to focus on her job, not the SEAL at the corner table.

Hell must have frozen over. And Jack sure as shit knew he was occupying prime real estate in the devil's inferno.

Spending twenty-four hours in Coronado, California with his older brothers was the definition of hell. But having the feisty Bottom's Up bartender come to his defense with an irresistible kiss, only for her to then leave him full with need as she walked into the back room?

It was heaven and hell all in one.

Most of the time, Natalie spotted him and walked away. He'd spent the past few years dreaming about her perfect ass and slim legs. But now Natalie's breasts would play a central role in his fantasies alongside her soft lips.

And she'd just slipped away from him.

"I'll be right back. Try not to pick a fight. Most of the men, and probably some of the women, could take you four against one." Without waiting for his brothers' comebacks, Jack pushed back from the table. He headed for the swinging double doors that separated the back room from the bar.

He scanned the employees-only space as the door closed behind him. Boxes, metal kegs, and an old popcorn machine filled the cramped space. Against one wall, he spotted the walk-in refrigerator. To the right was a long, narrow stainless steel table. Natalie stood with her back to him, her palms pressed against the silver surface and her chin dipped to her chest. Her long black hair fell forward, hiding her face.

She lifted one hand and smacked her palm against the table. Her hips rocked back, and when she bent at the waist, her spine formed a straight line. And all the blood in Jack's body moved south.

"Dammit," she muttered, hitting the table a second time. His brain processed the words, easily adding *Jack* to the end of her curse, followed by *harder*. But even with the blood rushing to his dick, he had a feeling he'd never hear the words *Dammit Jack, harder* cross her lips. Claiming the five-foot-two spitfire would remain his number one fantasy. He knew better than to assume one kiss would melt her hostility toward him.

Jack shoved his hands in the pockets of his cargo pants and crossed the small space. "Natalie?"

She glanced over her shoulder, her dark brown eyes daring him to take another step. "You shouldn't be back here."

"You know I can stand up for myself." Bypassing caution—hell, he routinely walked into volatile situations—Jack approached her. He stopped by her side, close enough to reach out and brush her long hair over her shoulder. His fingers pressed against his legs, eager for a green light. "Why'd you step in?"

"I hate bullies." She pushed off the table, turned to face him, and tilted her chin up.

"Me too. I appreciate what you did out there." He smiled at her, willing his feet to remain rooted to the floor while every cell in his body begged to reach for her. "Now I owe you one."

"No." She shook her head, black hair tumbling across her cheek. "I can stand up for myself, too. You don't owe me anything, Jack."

He cocked his head, studying the determined gleam in her eyes. "For a second back there, I thought you kind of liked me."

"You were wrong," she said firmly.

He withdrew his hands from his pockets and moved closer, half expecting her to back away. He towered over her petite frame, but she didn't give an inch.

"Do you rush in to defend a lot of men you don't like?" he asked, his voice soft and gentle, as though tempting a kitten out of hiding. "With a kiss?"

"I needed to shut your brothers up," she said.

"I like your approach." He reached out and took her hand. "Worked better than anything I tried as a kid."

Her lips curved into a small smile. "At least you fought back instead of running away."

"Natalie, I ran toward them. Once, I even beat Colton at

his own game."

She arched an eyebrow. "How?"

"I'll show you." He stepped forward. Natalie shifted away until her ass touched the table's edge, like she was following an unwritten rule stating that she needed to maintain a certain distance from him.

Jack paused. He offered her the chance to slip away and leave him facing a metal table. But she didn't move. He placed his hands on her bare shoulders, gliding his palms over her smooth skin. His jaw clenched, and hell if his cargo pants didn't feel as if they'd shrunk. He wrapped his fingers around her wrists and guided her arms behind her back.

"First, I pinned his arms behind his back," Jack murmured. He held her wrists with one hand, and he ran his fingers over her abdomen. A light, teasing touch through her clothes. Nothing more. "Then I tickled him until he begged for mercy."

"I won't beg," she said, her voice breathless.

"I know." He released her arms and lifted his hands to her face. "I'm just showing you my way. But I still like yours better."

Her hands moved to his chest, her fingers digging into his shirt. But she didn't push him away. He studied her face. Her brown eyes widened and her lips parted. He wanted another taste. It might end with her fist planted in his gut, but he was willing to take the risk.

He lowered his mouth to hers, allowing his fingers to weave through her long hair. With his eyes closed, he let his imagination run wild as his tongue tangled with hers. He pictured stripping away her clothes, climbing up on this table, and taking her. He wanted to tie her up, and it had nothing to do with his past. Hell, he wished he could claim the fantasy. Here. Now. Make her scream his name and acknowledge the fact that he'd made her come. Make her admit that part of her wanted him.

His lips sparred with hers, and he fought for control of the kiss. Natalie pressed her mouth hard against his. He stepped closer, his hands holding her head as his body touched her. Rocking his hips, he let her feel how much he wanted her.

She pushed back, breaking the kiss. "Is this how you say thank you?" she said, struggling to catch her breath. But the thread of steel he'd heard from across the bar night after night was there, loud and clear in her voice.

"No, ma'am." He released her long locks and ran his hands over her shoulders, down the side of her body, brushing the sides of her breasts. He wanted to memorize every inch of her, knowing she might never let him this close again. His hands wrapped around her waist.

"Is that what kind of man you are?" she breathed. "You don't even offer a woman a proper thank-you?"

"Natalie, if I was fixin' to offer a proper thank-you," he said, his Texas accent clear and present in his voice, "I'd kneel down right here and slide your jeans over your hips, down your damn-near perfect legs. I'd toss your pants across the room, followed by your panties. And then I'd lick you until the whole bar heard you come. Screaming. My. Name."

He released her hips and drew a path to the top closure of her jeans. His fingers toyed with the button as he stared into her wide brown eyes.

"Jack." Her hand covered his but stopped short of pushing him away.

"What do you say, Natalie? Would you like a proper thank-you?"

Chapter Two

Jack dominated her senses. She could taste his kiss on her lips. And she could smell the ocean on his skin, the scent mingling with spice. Not cologne. She couldn't picture the Navy SEAL splashing on the male version of perfume before leaving the house. This man didn't primp in front of the mirror. Everything about her Prince Charming was raw and unrefined.

Natalie blinked. *Her* prince? Not a chance. She refused to let his charm slip past her defenses and claim control of her.

"While this is impressive…" She slipped her hand between their bodies and pressed her palm against the hard bulge hidden behind his cargo pants. "A proper thank-you involves pen and paper, not—"

You. On your knees. Licking me.

Jack raised an eyebrow. "Not what?" he murmured, rocking his hips into her touch.

"You can't offer sex to everyone who saves you from a sticky situation," she snapped. She drew her hand away from his crotch. She shouldn't have touched him. Before she'd felt how much he had to offer beneath his pants, she'd clung to the illusion that the charming SEAL lobbed stupid pick-up lines across her bar night after night to compensate. One touch and that pipedream had vanished.

He tossed his head back and laughed. "Sure as hell would change my relationships with my teammates if I did," he said. "But to be clear, this thank-you would be designed for you."

Tell me more.

Her body craved details. The parts of her that knew it had been more than a year since her last hot, heavy, and not entirely satisfying encounter with a man, those parts needed more. Sixteen months was a long time without someone touching her, and the feel of her skin on Jack's left her wanting more, more, *more*. Where would he place his hands? Would his mouth live up to its sensual promise?

"This thank-you would be a one-of-a-kind expression of my gratitude that will leave you begging for more," he added.

"I never beg." Natalie leaned back against the table. She needed to escape and return to her customers. Details were dangerous, especially when they crossed this man's lips. Her gaze dropped to his mouth. He flashed his I-want-your-panties smile.

But if she handed over her underwear, she knew he'd ask for more and then walk away when she began to believe they might have a future together.

Rebellious. Stubborn. Her former foster parents' words echoed in her mind. After watching Jack from the other side of the bar, after tasting his kiss and feeling his hands wrap around her wrists, she had a feeling he'd like to replace defiant with submissive. And when she held her ground, he'd leave.

So that was how she'd get rid of him and save herself. If she was just herself—a challenge for a man like him—he'd give up on his own.

She pressed her hand against his chest, demanding space.

For a split second, he leaned into her touch.

"Never say never," he murmured. And then he obeyed her silent request, stepping back, offering the distance she needed to escape. "Never is a very long time, Natalie."

She blinked. She was on intimate terms with two things in her life—the vibrator in her nightstand and the word "never." At eleven, she'd lost her parents to a car crash. She'd been thrust into a world where she would *never* see them again. A world where she could *never* rely on anyone but herself as she and her sister moved from one foster family to the next. And she'd learned that she'd *never* feel entirely in control, not when she was with another person, no matter how hard she fought for it. Opening her heart, letting someone in, that was an invitation for heartbreak.

She moved to the door and stopped. One glance over her shoulder and she saw a glimmer of triumph in his blue eyes. Oh no, she refused to let him have the last word. "Jack?"

"Change your mind?"

She offered him a smile. "Never."

She pushed through the door and scanned the bar—four flirtatious fools, three tipsy blondes, two drunken sailors, and in the corner, Jack's brothers. But their party had grown, claiming a second table. Three of Jack's teammates sat with Colton and crew, including Cade Daniels, the man she'd considered her best friend long before the SEAL had proposed to her little sister.

Standing tall, she headed for the corner tables. She refused to let her customers see her unsettled from her conversation with Jack. And if anyone asked, she'd cling to her modified version of the truth—they'd been talking, end of story.

"Leave my little brother tied up?" Colton Barnes sneered.

Natalie withdrew her notepad and turned to Jack's teammates. "The usual, boys?"

Dante nodded. The Navy SEAL was a rugged warrior

whose coloring spoke of his mother's Italian heritage while his six-foot-plus frame left no doubt his father's side descended from Vikings. There was nothing boyish about him or Ronan, the red-haired, blue-eyed teammate sitting beside him.

"Are you okay?" Cade asked. The piercing look in his green eyes screamed *I heard you kissed Jack. Did you wake up with an extra dose of crazy this morning?*

"Fine." She stuffed her notepad into her apron.

Her best friend raised an eyebrow. "And Jack?"

"I was in the back, looking for a pen and paper," Jack said, rejoining the group, his carefree smile in place. "I came up empty." The man who'd kissed her senseless beside the broken Bottom's Up sign and popcorn maker turned to her. "Can I borrow yours?"

So he could spell out all of the tempting things she'd never do with him? Not a chance. "No."

She turned and headed for the bar, determined to do her job. The sooner she brought their drinks, the sooner they would leave her to tend to the mid-afternoon drunks and flirtatious fools. Out of the corner of her eye, she saw Jack claim a seat beside his teammates. He appeared relaxed, as though their kiss hadn't infused his body with an undeniable need.

Liar. I felt your cock—every hard, thick inch pressing against the palm of my hand.

She mentally slammed the door on that thought. Maybe she had woken up with an extra dose of crazy this morning. That would explain the impulse to kiss Jack Barnes. But right now, she needed to put her crazy to good use and pretend the charming Navy SEAL didn't measure up.

Jack forced a smile and pretended to listen as Ronan quizzed his brothers about raising cattle. His teammate's Irish accent—despite the fact that Ronan was born and raised in New York City—blended genuine interest with humor. And yeah, Colton was dumb enough to believe an officer with the SEAL teams wanted to hear about how to artificially inseminate a cow.

In his peripheral vision, he tracked Natalie's movements behind the bar. Her long hair swayed as she reached for a pint glass and set it beneath the taps. He wanted to wrap his hand around her long locks and make her beg for another kiss.

Never.

That one word she'd said echoed in his mind, his body ready and willing to accept that challenge and prove her wrong. Hell, most women followed him home without any effort on his part, and that was why he felt bored. But Natalie?

Never.

He was ready for a challenge. He was ready for Natalie.

"You can't hit that," Colton leered, kicking Jack under the table just like when they sat down to one of his mom's home-cooked masterpieces at the Barnes ranch. Growing up, his brothers had taken every chance to land a hit.

Dante glanced at him, eyebrow raised. "Are you making a serious play for Natalie?"

"He'd never get her into bed," Colton said. "I'm willing to put money on it. Mom said you were taking a few days off, without bothering to visit her—"

"Cade's getting married," Jack shot back. "I'm the best man in his wedding this weekend. I talked to Mom. She understood."

Out of the corner of his eye, Jack saw Natalie, who'd be playing the part of the maid of honor, carry the filled tray out from behind the bar. She headed in their direction but came to an abrupt stop ten paces away when a young blonde nearly tumbled out of her chair trying to get Natalie's attention.

"I bet you can't get the bartender into your bed by the time you ship out again," his big brother said, pretending Jack hadn't offered an explanation for skipping a trip home to see his parents while he had a few days leave.

"Fifty bucks," Colton added. "Anyone else want in?"

Jack glanced at Natalie as the pack of Barnes brothers reached for their wallets. Her eyes widened, but she kept her smile in place while she talked to her customers. Had she heard Colton's proposal? At Jack's table, a chorus of "hell yeahs" filled their corner of the bar as money was slapped on the table.

Dante shook his head. "I won't put money on it, but Jack, man, you don't stand a chance. Natalie doesn't even like you. Right, Cade? She's your friend. You know her better than any of us."

"Leave me out of this," Cade said, stealing a quick glance at Natalie. His teammate could read Natalie better than anyone here. And judging from the way he shook his head, Cade knew the Bottom's Up bartender was close to spitting fire even while she nodded at something the blonde said.

"Your guy here knows you can't do it," Colton said with a laugh. Then his brother turned to Ronan. "What about you? Are you in?"

Ronan's blue eyes narrowed and his smile faded. It seemed his teammate had just realized that Jack wished his brothers had remained on the family ranch, dealing with the cow semen. "My money's on Jack. I've never witnessed a situation he couldn't handle."

"You're throwing away fifty bucks," Dante murmured. "Jack's the first person I want covering my six, watching my back, on a mission. But if Natalie wanted him, she'd have claimed him years ago."

"Claimed him?" Colton kicked him under the table again

as the rest of his family laughed. "Down in Texas, we go after our women. We don't wait for them to come to us."

Bullshit.

But there was a spark of truth buried in his big brother's challenge. He'd wanted Natalie for six long years. And yeah, he'd spent a large part of that time deployed, but still, wasn't it about time he went after the woman who filled his fantasies?

"What do you say, kid?" Colton prodded.

"I'm in," Jack said, unwilling to walk away from his brother's challenge. He didn't lose. Not to Colton Barnes. Not anymore. And shit, after the way Natalie had kissed him, touched him—dammit, he wanted to turn her *never* into *Yes, Jack. Give me more.* "Before the bride walks down the aisle, I'll have her in my bed."

And she wouldn't claim him. His jaw jumped and the tension rippled through his seemingly relaxed body. No, he'd make her *his*, take control, ignite the passion and need he'd tasted in her kiss—

Natalie set her filled tray on their table. "Jack Barnes, prepare to lose your money." She placed her hands on her hips. "Because as much as I hate to side with Mr. Belt Buckle here," she waved her hand at Colton, "nothing you say will talk me out of my clothes and into your bed. Pick someone else to seduce, sailor."

Shit. Had she heard *everything*? Well, that would make this interesting.

"Nothing?" Jack fought the flush threatening to turn his cheeks fucking pink with embarrassment in front of his brothers. He stared into Natalie's dark brown eyes and searched for a sign that he'd offended her by taking the bet. And thank you Jesus, he came up empty.

"Nothing. You know I hate bullies," she said with a pointed look at Colton. "But you can't win this one."

"That sounds like a challenge," Jack said. "And Natalie, I

always play to win."

"I dare you to try," she shot back.

He stood and stepped in front of her. He heard her sharp inhale as he placed one finger under her chin and tilted her head back, her fiery, take-no-prisoners gaze meeting his. He scanned her eyes, looking for anger. As a rule, he liked an even playing field, not a cornered opponent. He'd filled those shoes as a kid and tried damn hard never to place anyone else in that position—terrorists excluded.

But if hearing about the bet had pissed her off at first, her competitive spirit had risen and displaced her anger. Studying her face, he saw a woman determined to win and to battle their mutual attraction. And yeah, that kiss earlier had proven he wasn't the only one interested in taking their relationship to a new level. Not that anyone would define their verbal sparring—when she wasn't flat-out ignoring him—as a relationship.

"Game on," he said, smiling down at her. "Game on."

Chapter Three

Monday night had threatened to drive her crazy between Jack's brothers and that stupid bet. But Tuesday's shift just might break her.

She turned her back to the bar and wrapped her hand around the Jack that promised comfort—and nothing more—for the weeping sailor at the far end of the bar.

Her grip tightened around the bottle as she glanced over her shoulder at her crying customer. Jack Daniels' brand of comfort would leave the young man with a wicked hangover, and in the morning, he'd still have the pain of losing his best friend.

She quietly set the bottle in front of the young man and his friend perched on the barstool beside him mainlining water. But the crying sailor's designated driver eyed the Jack Daniels.

"Have a drink with your friend," she said. "And I'll call you a cab at the end of the night."

The sober sailor gave a curt nod. "Thank you, ma'am."

"Natalie," she corrected as someone at the far end of the

bar called her name. She left the young men, turned toward the familiar voice, and braced for a melt-your-panties-off smile from the Jack that left her weaker than a whole bottle of liquor.

Jack Barnes—the Jack in her life who'd made a bet that he could claim a place in her bed—waved to her as he claimed a stool. She headed for the opposite end of the long, wooden bar. She stopped directly in front of him and placed her hands on her hips. "Don't start with me tonight, Jack. You're not going to win. But if you try…"

Her thoughts traveled down the length of the bar to the crying sailor. When the sailor first dissolved into tears, the former designated driver had whispered an explanation. The weeping sailor had flown back from the Middle East with one hand on his best friend's casket. They'd enlisted together, fought together, but only one of them had come home.

"Not tonight," she said, fighting to hide the tremor in her voice.

"How about a beer?" he asked, his smile fading. "While I cheer you up."

She shook her head and turned to the taps to pour his usual. She doubted Prince Charming could remove the weight resting on her shoulders. She knew grief and loss. The crying sailor's pain wouldn't vanish after a long visit with Jack Daniels. It would be there tomorrow when he woke up.

She pressed the lever and stopped the flow of beer before Prince Charming's cup overflowed. Glancing down the bar, she watched the teary-eyed sailor down another shot. She should probably cut the kid off and send him home now. Lessen the headache in the morning even if she couldn't fix the heartache of losing his best friend.

"One more shot, kid," she murmured. And then she turned to the other side of the bar—and bit back a growl.

A woman who looked like she'd walked off the set of a

country music video and headed for Bottom's Up went for the empty stool beside Jack. The click of her cowgirl boots on the bar's wooden floor announced her approach. And Jack gave the woman his full attention. Natalie could practically see him running through a mental checklist.

Cutoff jean shorts that bordered on indecent? Yes.

Fitted white T-shirt over her red, white, and blue bikini top? Uh-huh.

Warm, welcoming, I'll-hand-you-my-panties-after-one-drink smile?

Natalie cocked her head and studied the red-haired, green-eyed beauty as she removed her cowboy hat and claimed the empty stool. The woman's smile was shy but guarded, almost like she'd selected that particular stool in spite of Jack, not because of him.

A handful of her regulars glanced at the newcomer too, and for a second Natalie wondered if the woman might be someone slightly famous. Thanks to her lack of cable TV, all the housewives in Orange County could parade through her bar and Natalie wouldn't have a clue.

She headed over to deliver Jack's drink and watched as the woman's shy veneer vanished. The redhead's lips parted and her eyes widened.

Natalie froze, still holding Jack's beer. She could deliver it, turn, and walk away. Or—

"Oh, wow, you're a Navy SEAL. Your job must be so *hard*," the woman said.

Or she could listen to Jack pick up the newcomer. Her jaw tightened. That was just what this night needed.

"Some days it's tough," Jack admitted. "Today gave me a headache. But I hear sex cures headaches. Want to give it a shot?"

She walked over and slammed his beer down on the bar, interrupting before the California Cowgirl could offer a breathy "yes" and drag Jack out the door. She didn't want Prince Charming driving her crazy from one end of the bar while the sad, miserable sailor at the other end left her wishing she could escape to the back for a long, hard cry—but she hated the thought of him "curing" his headache with the redhead.

"I'll take your money now if you're headed out," Natalie said, trying for a matter-of-fact, I-don't-care-if-you-bang-the-cowgirl tone. She failed. But damn if something that felt an awful lot like jealousy was nipping at her heels.

Because twenty-four hours ago, U.S. Navy SEAL Jack Barnes had kissed *her*. He'd bet on *her*. She refused to let him win. But still—

"We're not going anywhere just yet," Jack said. "Miss Casey, would you like a beer?"

Casey the Cowgirl shook her head. "A shot of tequila, please. I think I need to start tonight off with something strong."

Natalie spun around, not waiting until the redhead's gaze lingered over Jack's powerful biceps. She should probably do them both a favor and tell Casey that subtlety wasn't necessary with Mr. Sex Cures Headaches. They didn't need to hang out at her bar and get smashed before they left together. And dammit, the last thing Natalie needed on her final shift before heading to Vegas was a bar full of drunks.

She pressed her lips together as she poured the shot, trying to beat back the green-eyed, jealous monster. Slim chance. When had fate ever given her what she needed?

"Thank you," Jack said to the young woman who looked like she'd taken a detour on the road to Nashville. "For playing along."

"My pleasure," Casey said, toying with her cowgirl hat. "But I'm not sure jealousy is the way to go. She looks angry."

"Yup," he agreed, raising his glass and taking a sip. He kept his gaze fixed on Natalie, watching her abrupt movements as she poured the tequila. No doubt about it, the bartender was pissed at him. But he'd rather see her spitting mad at him than looking like she was on the verge of tears.

And when he'd sat down tonight, the woman who defined feisty 364 days of the year looked as if her dog had died. Shit, Jack had been tempted to text Cade and ask if Mufasa, the dog his teammate co-owned with Natalie, was all right. He could have pressed Natalie for details, but he suspected she'd pour his drink over his head before having a heart-to-heart with him.

"Trying to win the bet before we hit Vegas?" Ronan's voice interrupted his thoughts.

"No." Jack set his beer down on the bar. He wasn't "winning" anything tonight. Natalie had been clear on that, and judging from the rowdy Tuesday night crowd, she was in for a long shift.

She picked up the tequila shot and rushed over. She set it down in front of Casey and glanced at his teammate. "The usual, Ronan?"

"When you get a chance," his teammate said.

She nodded and turned to the lineup of people calling her name and shouting out drink orders. But instead of pointing to one and saying, *You're first, what are you having*, she glanced toward the end of the bar.

"Hold your horses," she called to the crowd as she headed for the young man balling his eyes out over a shot glass. A bottle of the hard stuff sat in front of him.

"She's not having a good night," Jack said. And then he watched as she covered the crying man's hand with her own. She leaned across the bar until her forehead was practically touching the man bent over his shot glass.

"I think you might have a better chance if you pretend to cry," Casey said. She raised her tequila to her lips and took a sip. "Might work better than trying to make her angry and jealous."

Behind his left shoulder, Ronan let out a loud laugh. "Jack doesn't need to try to make Natalie angry. He's a natural. But jealous? I wish I'd seen that."

Casey glanced over her shoulder, and her eyes widened as she caught sight of Jack's teammate. "I love your accent," she murmured.

"Ronan, take my stool." Jack stood, abandoning the beer he'd barely touched. "I'm going to see if Natalie needs a hand."

Knowing the wandering cowgirl would enjoy his replacement far more—even though the chances of the SEAL officer taking Casey home were slim to none due to his no one-night stands rule—Jack headed for the opposite end of the bar.

Natalie had slipped away to serve her demanding customers, but the man whose hand she'd been holding was silently shaking as tears rolled down his face. His friend sat beside him, equally grim.

"Hey man," Jack said to the stone-faced friend. "Everything all right?"

The guy glanced at him. "He's taking the loss hard."

Jack assumed a parade rest position, hands clasped behind his back as the whole story poured out.

"Jack, leave them alone," Natalie said, her voice breathless from rushing around the bar and filling orders. She placed her palms flat on the bar.

"It's all right," he said. "I'm not harassing the kid. I'm going to take them home."

Her eyes widened. "What about your new friend?"

"She's in good hands." He helped the drunken sailor off the stool, holding the man close to his side to keep him from falling down. "I wasn't interested in her, Natalie." He looked up and saw the blatant disbelief in Natalie's sharp gaze.

"But—"

"I want you, Natalie. And I have the entire weekend to prove it to you."

Chapter Four

"Is this your idea of revenge?" Natalie demanded, her cell pressed to her ear as she stared at the fuchsia abomination hanging on the door to her bedroom closet.

"Cade dropped off the dress?" her little sister asked mildly.

"Your fiancé dropped off the dress and ran away before I unzipped the enormous garment bag," Natalie said. "Coward."

Lucia laughed. "You don't like it?"

"No." Natalie eyed the fluffy pink dress that looked like something a ballerina would wear to play the part of the wedding cake, not the maid of honor. Having never set foot in a ballet class, Natalie had never been this close to so much tulle. It felt ominous and threatening. And she wondered if the hideous dress just might eat her alive.

"But that was the point, wasn't it?" Natalie continued. "You wanted revenge."

Fourteen months ago, Lucia had gone to Vegas to pick up a stranger at a masquerade party. Natalie's little sister had planned on one wild night with a man who would never glimpse beneath her mask and see the jagged, awful scars left by their third and final foster father. Of course, the scars wouldn't be a part of Lucia's life if Natalie hadn't defied their foster parents' authority and slipped away from the house.

Natalie closed her eyes as the familiar guilt washed over her. She should have been there to protect Lucia. When she received an email from her sister about her Vegas plans, Natalie had stepped in, determined to keep her sister safe. She'd failed the last time. But she would do everything she could to keep Lucia from being hacked to pieces and left in the desert by an ax murderer.

Not that all men looking for a wild night in Vegas were ax murderers. Just like most foster parents would never hurt the children placed in their care, most of the men interested in a single woman probably wanted a night of no-strings-attached sex. But when it came to her sister, Natalie refused to leave Lucia's safety to chance. Because Lucia's scars proved that if you gambled and lost, you could end up with the drunken jerk that would take a knife to a teenager's face.

So she'd asked her best friend Cade, who was planning to visit his dad in Vegas anyway, to look out for Lucia. And he'd done exactly that from a very close proximity—Lucia's bed. And because Cade had his own issues, he hadn't told Lucia that he'd gone to Vegas to find her.

In the end, Lucia forgave Natalie. But her little sister had promised she'd seek revenge—and Natalie was looking right at it.

"Lucia, are you sure that you want me to stand at the altar in this dress?" Natalie said. "There are ways to get revenge that won't distract the guests' attention from you in your wedding gown."

Her sister laughed again, driving home the fact that her newfound happiness bubbled over at the drop of a hat. If she didn't love Lucia more than anyone on earth, or have an up close and personal understanding of what her sister had gone through prior to landing in Happily Ever After Land, Natalie might feel a bit jealous.

But when Natalie closed her eyes, she saw the fresh wounds on her sister's face. And guilt sent the green-eyed monster running for the hills.

"It's a friends and family Vegas wedding," Lucia said as her laughter faded. "The entire event promises to be a little wild and crazy. Plus, I don't care if everyone else stares at you. Cade will be looking at me. And that's all that matters."

"Okay. But after this we're even, right?"

"Maybe," Lucia said. "I also have one small favor to ask you."

"Favor?" Natalie ran her hand over the tutu on steroids, which puffed out from the fitted strapless and satin bodice. "I'm not sure you're in any position to ask for a favor."

"They make the dress in this weird sherbet orange color. I could order—"

"Maid of honor reporting for duty," Natalie said quickly. Any favor was preferable to a sherbet orange dress. "How can I help you?"

"Jack's truck broke down. He was planning to drive to Vegas today, too. Can you give him a ride?"

Natalie closed her eyes. Five, maybe six hours in a car with Texas's very own Prince Charming, the man hell-bent on talking his way into her bed. The man who kissed like a god...

"No. My poor little compact car is already full. I'll have Mufasa in the backseat," she said, referring to the Great Pyrenees she co-owned with Cade. "And this dress has to hang somewhere. I don't have room for six feet plus of Navy SEAL."

"He's not a big guy," Lucia said. "Sure, he's tall. But he's lean and trim. I'm sure parts of him are small."

Not his cock.

Her cheeks heated at the memory of Jack's very long, hard, and most definitely *big* length pressed against her hand.

"Parts of who are small?" Natalie heard Cade's deep voice in the background, followed by the sound of a door closing.

"Please say yes," Lucia said, ignoring her fiancé. "I need to go. Cade and I have something we need to do. Wedding things."

More like practice for the wedding night.

Natalie shook her head, trying to dislodge that thought. "Fine. I'll drive him. But I'm leaving at noon today. If he's not here, I'm hitting the road without him. He pays for half the gas."

And if he thinks for even a second that this brings him closer to winning the bet, he's wrong.

She didn't dare say the words out loud. Lucia didn't know about the bet. Natalie had promised Cade she'd tell her sister, but she couldn't bring herself to say anything. Not now. Not yet.

If she breathed a word about Jack's challenge, Lucia would step in and put a stop to the bet before Natalie could see Jack struggle. And Natalie didn't want that. She was going to beat him at his own game.

Cade hated keeping secrets from his fiancée, but Natalie would tell her after the wedding, after Jack had lost, and after he'd shipped out again.

Natalie ended the call and stared at the Terrible Tutu as a plan formed in her mind. Maybe she could use this drive to crush Jack's plans before they reached the state line.

With his rucksack over one shoulder, Jack stood on the sidewalk outside Natalie's apartment complex and watched as she wrestled a bright pink monster into her trunk.

"You know, the moment I first saw you behind the bar, I knew you would be fun," he drawled. "But I never pictured you in pink."

Natalie glanced over her shoulder, both hands still buried in the pink thing. If that was her idea of a dress…shit, he'd take her shopping when they hit Vegas. And visiting women's clothing stores was possibly the last item on his list of Things To Do With Natalie. Or next to last, right above shoe shopping. But that pink thing—

"Your idea of fun is staring at my back while I ignore you?" she said.

"Yes." His gaze shifted to her ass. If they were alone, out of sight of her neighbors and the possibility that a cop could drive by and arrest them for indecent exposure, he would order her to spread her legs and keep her hands planted. He pictured moving behind her and pressing up against her. He would lean forward and draw her shirt up, exposing her bra. Then he'd run his hands over her bare skin until he reached her skirt. He would draw the fabric up, revealing her panties inch by inch. Then he would leave the bunched-up material decorating her hips. He'd run his hands up her butt and explore every inch of her. And she wouldn't move without his permission.

Another woman would follow his orders. But not Natalie. Not yet. And he didn't want anyone else.

"We have different ideas of fun," she said.

"Oh, I think we'd agree on some things. Give me a chance and I'll prove it."

"No." She quickly released the pink monster and slammed the trunk. A small piece of the skirt had slipped out and was now dangling over her bumper. "Your bag will have to ride in the backseat with Mufasa," she added.

Jack nodded as he approached the compact black car. He opened the rear passenger side door and slid his rucksack along the floor. The Great Pyrenees lying across the seat lifted his head and glanced at the bag.

He gently closed the door, leaving the giant dog to mourn his fate — a long drive in a small, overfilled car. He moved to the passenger side door and opened it. "Hop in, Natalie, and I promise to drive you wild."

"No, you won't." She headed for the driver's side. "My car. I'm driving. And I brought earphones."

"Worried I'll seduce you on the highway?" He settled into the passenger seat, trying to recall the last time he rode shotgun. As a rule, he drove. His teammates all respected the fact that he'd excelled at defense driving/race car school. And he liked being in control of the vehicle.

"No, but I have a feeling you'll give me a headache with all of your stupid pick-up lines." She turned the key and slipped the car in reverse.

"I've heard sex cures headaches."

Natalie kept her gaze focused on the road. "I heard you use that one last night, Jack."

"Not on you."

"Oh, wow, you're a Navy SEAL. Your job must be so *hard*," she said, raising her voice an octave in a decent imitation of the redhead he'd met at Bottom's Up yesterday. "Some days it's tough," she continued, lowering her voice. But shit, he didn't sound like that. Not even close. "Today gave me a headache. But I hear sex cures headaches. Want to give it a shot?"

"It worked," he pointed out. "If I hadn't turned her attention to Ronan, she would have volunteered to help with my headache."

Natalie laughed as she merged onto the highway. "Most women see your smile and tumble into your bed. They're not even listening when you deliver your lines comparing them to aspirin."

"But you're listening," he said. "Even when you're pretending to ignore me."

"It's part of the job." She shifted in her seat, her skirt riding up her thighs. "I pay attention to everything that happens in my bar."

Jack fought the urge to reach over and rest his hand on her thigh. She'd probably swerve into the breakdown lane and slam on the brakes. Then she'd demand that he get out of the car and walk to Sin City.

"Stop staring at my legs, Jack."

"It's a nice skirt," he said. "Can I talk you out of it?"

"Sure." She glanced over her left shoulder and moved into the passing lane.

He coughed, his eyes widening.

Well shit, that was easy. Too easy—

"I'll change into jeans at the next rest stop," she added.

He laughed and glanced out the window. They sped past a semi and a driver who'd mistaken the highway bypassing Los Angeles for a two-lane road in a school zone. But Natalie didn't move back into the right-hand lane.

"In a hurry to get there?" he asked.

"Lucia put me in charge of the bachelorette party. I have a long to-do list. And before you ask, no, having sex with you in your bed, my bed, or anywhere else is not on that list. You're not getting laid tonight, so you can stop with the lines."

"Tomorrow, tomorrow, I love ya tomorrow," he sang, not bothering to match the high pitch of the little girl who'd made the lyrics famous. "You're only—"

"Please," she said, her tone raw and rough, nothing like the I'm-pretending-to-be-annoyed tone she'd used since they left Coronado. "I hate that song."

He shut up and studied her profile. The corner of her full lips dipped into a frown. He wished he could erase the sorrow from her expression. But shit, he'd caused it by not making the connection between little orphan Annie and the woman who'd lost her parents to a car accident. "Sorry."

"Tomorrow isn't always better," she said, her hands clutching the steering wheel, her knuckles turning white.

"No, it isn't," he said. "But I still try to hold on to that hope. Because looking back at the past? That sucks, too."

She slammed on the brakes, and his gaze snapped to the red lights stretching on and on in front of them. Sirens sounded, the noise growing closer. Seconds later, emergency vehicles sped past them in the breakdown lane.

Shit. Perfect timing for a freaking accident. Not that there was a good time for a car crash—

"There's an accident ahead," she murmured as the vehicle in front of them moved an inch and stopped.

"It just happened," he said. "This place is like a parking lot. And we still have hours to go."

Accidents sucked. And sitting in traffic wasn't at the top of his list of fun things to do, but…

"Looks like we'll be here for a while," he added with a playful smile, turning to her.

"Yes," she said, closing her eyes as though she wished to block out the scene in front of them.

His smile vanished. Shit, was she envisioning the turned over cars? Was her mind traveling back in time to the accident that killed her parents? He reached out and gave her shoulder a squeeze. "Are you all right, Natalie?"

She opened her eyes. "I'm just… I'm…"

The giant dog whimpered from the backseat, shifting his massive weight. And her gaze narrowed as if she'd just returned to here and now inside her compact car. She shrugged his hand off her shoulder.

"I'm just worried about Mufusa," she said. She lifted her hips and reached her right arm back to pet her four-legged friend. The move caused her skirt to slide up her legs.

Jack stared at the bare, smooth skin. It would be a while before she changed into those jeans.

"Jack," she said, her tone heavy with warning as she settled back into her seat.

"I know, I know." He turned to look out the window and grinned. He'd rather have her sparring with him than lost in the past. "I'll stop looking. But every time I close my eyes, I'll picture running my hands and lips over your smooth skin. Touching you. Tasting you—"

"I've been sitting in this hot car with you and a dog for the past hour," she shot back. "I'm sweaty. I wouldn't taste good."

"Yes, Natalie. You would. Trust me." Just thinking about what she would feel like against his tongue, the sounds she would make when she finally surrendered to pleasure—hell, his imagination might drive him crazy before they reached Nevada.

Chapter Five

Fate was on a mission to prove that her luck hadn't changed. They'd spent three hours parked on the highway around Los Angeles while workers cleared away the accident. This brought their total time spent in her very compact car up to six hours.

Natalie steered the car into the parking lot of a two-story motel located in middle of nowhere California. If they kept going on the two-lane country road, they'd hit the California-Nevada state line before dark. But Mufasa was growing restless. And Natalie was dying for a break.

The drive had shaken her. When they'd inched up to the scene, she'd spotted the totaled passenger car on the side of the road and the tractor-trailer lying on its side. Maybe the truck driver had survived. But the passengers in the smashed car?

A shiver ran down her spine. Earlier, when they'd drawn to a stop, she'd closed her eyes, haunted by fear for the crash victims and their families. And Jack had placed his hand on her shoulder.

Now, the memory of that touch and his concern haunted her. She knew he wanted her in his bed. He wanted to win the bet. That was fine. Desire and seduction she could deal with. Probably even resist. But knowing he actually cared? That chipped away at her resolve and left her wanting him. Just a little.

But not enough to let him win.

"Do you want me to go inside and secure a room in the back?" Jack asked. "You can drive around and let Mufasa out to stretch his legs."

"Sure, but get two rooms. I'm not sharing a bedroom with a man who made a bet to seduce me."

"Are you sure? I don't mind sharing."

She let out a laugh. Of course he didn't mind. He probably saw it as bringing her a step closer to victory.

"Sometimes these out-of-the-way motels charge more than they're worth," he added. "Because they're the only game in town."

She quickly calculated the cash in her purse—most of which she had allocated for bachelorette party favors—and came up short even for a room in the middle of nowhere.

He studied her, and for a second she wondered if he could read her mind. "One room would save us both a few bucks. Destination weddings aren't cheap."

Unless they were giving rooms away, she'd have to charge tonight's stay. And pray she didn't go over her credit card limit when she handed over her card to the hotel in Vegas. Not a possibility she wanted to face.

Besides, what was the harm in staying in one room for one night with Jack? She could use it to her advantage. Show him that staying in one room together didn't matter. She wasn't going to let him touch her. She wasn't going to let him kiss her. She wasn't going to let him—

"Okay," she said. "One room. With two beds. And I need

your word that you'll behave."

"I don't make promises I can't keep." He opened the passenger side door. "I'll get the two beds. But darlin', I'm hoping you'll give one to the dog."

Natalie sipped her strawberry milkshake and stared out the diner window at the motel across the street. "We should have placed a to-go order. Mufasa is probably lonely."

"Will he tear up the room?" Jack asked. "Or bark until the entire motel knows he's there?"

She shook her head. "No, he'll behave. Cade trained him well."

"Cade spends about sixty days a year with his dog. *You* trained him well."

"Well, Cade's the one who trained me," Natalie shot back, refusing the compliment.

She shook her head at herself. Why couldn't she accept his praise? For training her dog for goodness sake.

Because smiling and saying thank you was tantamount to letting down her guard. She might as well let him pin her wrists behind her back and kiss her again. But one kiss and she'd be toast. The charming Navy SEAL—the man who'd proved he cared about her dammit—he would ravage her mouth and melt her resolve.

Steer clear! Stay in control! Don't trust anyone else!

The rules for her life would fly out the window.

Across the table, Jack raised an eyebrow. "Good to know you can take instruction."

Thankfully, the waitress chose that moment to skate up to the table and deliver their burgers along with a giant basket of fries.

"Watching the servers in this place, I'm glad I don't have

to wear a pair of roller-skates and a short skirt to deliver drinks," she said, reaching for the ketchup. "I'd get more than a wink and stupid come-on lines when new guys dropped by. Maybe even from the regulars. Though they mostly behave themselves now."

Except you, Jack.

"Because they've seen you take on ten misbehaving Marines," he pointed out before sinking his teeth into his burger.

"Hasn't stopped you," she countered.

"No, but you find me charming." But his hand-over-your-panties grin quickly faded. "And I'm sorry about my brothers. My mom did her best, trying to raise them right. But five boys running wild on a cattle ranch proved to be too much."

"Are your parents still in Texas?"

He nodded. "They all live on the ranch. I think Mom likes having most of her brood close even if they are a little wild."

"That sounds nice," she said, fighting back emotion. One car crash had altered her future, erasing the possibility of a family home where her parents would welcome her back during the holidays.

"I take it for granted, focusing on the parts I hated about growing up the youngest. And Colton was right." He paused and set his burger down. He raised his right hand and ran his fingers through his short hair, his muscles flexing and threatening to distract her from his words. "Jesus, I can't believe I said those words."

"I won't tell Colton," she said, looking away from his arm. "What was Mr. Belt Buckle right about?"

"My older brother nailed it when he said I was scrawny as a kid. Sometimes, in my head, I still feel like that weak boy who needs to fight back."

She reached for her milkshake. This man possessed the kind of muscles male underwear models dreamed about when they hit the gym. And his biceps came from fighting the bad guys, training to be the best and save the world. But she couldn't tell him that. Right now, she couldn't even find the words to tease him.

"The accident today," he said, his tone surprisingly serious.

Oh no. The Prince Charming of the Navy SEALs didn't do deep and thoughtful. Did he?

"Please. We don't need to—"

"It hit close to home, didn't it?" he asked. "Cade told me about how you lost your parents."

"Yes." She let go of her milkshake and stared at her plate, unable to say another word. The feelings were too big, too powerful. The sadness and anger would tear through her control. And she refused to rip the Band-Aid off her emotional scars over burgers with the man who had bet that he could seduce her.

She could fantasize about stripping off Jack's T-shirt, undoing his cargo pants, and reaching inside to stroke his hard length. While she lay in bed with her battery-operated friend, she could close her eyes and dream about the naughty things he'd described in the back room of her bar after he'd kissed her. She could imagine his tongue teasing her clit and his cock thrusting into her as she mimicked the motions with her toy in the real world.

But she drew the line at liking Jack Barnes. She couldn't open up to the charmer. She'd considered Cade her best friend for years, and there was so much she'd never shared with him—about the night Lucia was attacked, about her own lingering feelings of guilt, about her fear of letting anyone too close. Sure, that had come back to haunt her when Cade had discovered how living in foster care had literally scarred her little sister. But Natalie refused to show anyone what it had done to her on the inside.

She turned away from him. "I'm going to take my burger

to go," she said, wrapping it in a napkin. "The milkshake filled me up, and Mufasa would love this."

"Natalie, I'm sorry," he said quietly.

She felt his blue eyes on her, tracking her movements as she grabbed her purse, then withdrew a twenty-dollar bill and tossed it on the table. "You don't have to apologize. I just need to see my dog. Make sure he hasn't claimed one of the beds. I'd hate for you to have to sleep on the floor."

She slid out of the booth and headed for the door leading to fresh air and emotional safety.

J ack watched Natalie wait for a break in traffic before she raced across the two-lane road to their motel. He stayed focused on her, waving away the waitress when she rolled by to check on him. After Natalie disappeared around the corner, he turned back to his meal. The burger was pretty damn good, but his appetite had walked out the door with his dinner date. Not that this was a real date, but—

Fuck, I can't even tempt her to share a burger with me. How the hell am I going to talk her into kissing me again?

Maybe it was just lust before he deployed again for God knew how long, but so what if it was? He'd wanted her for too damn long to walk away from her just yet. And he sure as hell wasn't letting his brothers and teammates win the bet.

He picked up his burger. He'd eat, giving her a little time and space before he returned to their shared room. Before he went back to the woman who'd played a leading role in his fantasies. And hell, she had given him reason to believe he'd starred in a few of her fantasies when she'd kissed him at her bar. Maybe it was finally time to turn those fantasies into reality.

Chapter Six

As the sun dipped below the horizon, Jack slipped into the hotel room and found Natalie curled up on one of the queen-sized beds watching TV. Her giant dog had claimed a corner of the room where Natalie had laid out towels as a makeshift bed. When they'd brought their stuff in earlier, she'd mumbled something about letting Mufasa sleep on the pink dress in the trunk. The dog would probably ruin it, and then she wouldn't have to wear it to the wedding. He saw the merits to her plan, but she'd left the pink monster locked in the car.

"What are you watching?" he asked, sitting on the edge of the unoccupied bed. He finished unlacing his boots and slipped the clunky black shoes off.

"A reality show," she said. "I don't have a TV, so I have no idea what's happening. I pick up some celebrity gossip at the bar, but…"

On the screen, two women in evening gowns lunged for each other.

"I'm guessing the guys who drop in for a drink or two after

a long day on the base aren't exactly up-to-date on this stuff," he said, removing his second boot. He kept his eyes on the scene as the catfight continued. "But they might change their minds if the producers put the girls in bikinis and transitioned this scene to a giant pool of Jell-O."

"I don't think that's where this is headed," she murmured. "But the group date is coming up next, and all of these ladies want that rose, so it's possible. I can't believe all of these women are dating this one guy."

"What if he decides he wants more than one?" He leaned back and rested on his hands. "Can't he just say 'let's have a threesome' and pick his two favorites?"

"I don't think so. And even if he did, I think the sex happens off screen."

"Disappointed?"

She laughed and picked up the remote. "No, I'm not into voyeurism." She hit a button and the TV went dark. "We should get ready for bed. I'd like to leave first thing in the morning. Mufasa will need to go out again. The less moving him in and out of the room, the better. And we need to get to Vegas in time for the wedding party meet and greet by the pool."

She slipped off the bed, grabbed a pile of clothes off the dresser, and escaped into the bathroom.

Shit. Natalie wasn't into voyeurism. That tidbit did him a helluva lot of good. Not that he was crazy about voyeurism either, but he needed to know what she was into, what turned her on and left her wet and wanting.

He ran his hand over his face and stood, moving to his rucksack to dig out his toothbrush. Right now, it was damn hard to believe he'd earned a reputation as the team charmer. But after they turned out the lights, he was ready to give his floundering seduction another shot.

Ten minutes later, Natalie turned off the lamp on the

nightstand nestled between their beds and plunged the room into darkness. A loud rumbling sound filled the space, punctuated by the occasional snort. Shit, nothing said "let's get it on" like a one-hundred pound snoring dog.

Oh no sweetheart, I'm not going to let you shut me down that easily.

"I get not wanting to watch," he said. "But what about listening?"

"To other people having sex?" she said. "To their weird noises?"

"No." He turned on his side and propped himself up on one elbow. Even in the dark room, he could make out the outline of her body covered in blankets on the other bed. "And why would you assume their noises would be weird?"

"I think all sex noises are strange," she said.

He'd like a chance to prove her wrong on that front. But first he had to find out what turned her on. Maybe her kinks led to strange sounds.

"We have a few hours in the car tomorrow," he said. "You can explain your theory in detail."

"I don't think so—"

"But right now, I'm offering you a bedtime story."

He saw the outline of her body shift as she turned on her side. He couldn't quite make out her face, but he sensed she was looking at him.

"You're going to tell me a sexy bedtime story?" she said. And she sounded amused, which sure as shit beat the dark cloud he'd brought over their conversation in the diner.

"Yes."

"That's how you plan to seduce me?" she said. "It won't work. There's no way you're going to win me over with the power of your words. I'm not going to succumb to the sound of your voice and change my mind about having sex with you tonight. Or any night," she quickly added.

A little too quickly, he thought.

"When was the last time someone told you a dirty story?" he asked, his voice dropping low. "A story so naughty you wanted to slip your hand under your clothes and touch yourself?"

"Never."

"Do you dare me to try?"

"Yes," she said in a soft, breathy tone he'd never heard her use while tending bar. "I want the chance to prove you wrong. This won't work. And I want an original, not a recycled story that you used to talk your way into some girl's pants."

"I've never done this before," he admitted. She'd been right in the car when she said most women fell easily into his bed. But Natalie was far from easy. And damn if that didn't turn him on.

"You're a storytelling virgin?" she teased.

"I am." He sat up, resting his back against the headboard fixed to the motel room wall. "Now, lie on your back and close your eyes. I promise I'll be more entertaining than the girls fighting on TV."

He waited until her outline shifted in the darkness, the covers moving over her body. Beneath the thin motel blanket, she wore sweatpants and a baggy gray Navy T-shirt that looked like it had once been a part of Cade's limited wardrobe. The minute she'd walked out of the bathroom, he'd wanted her out of those clothes.

"I'm ready," she said. "Let's hear your story."

He stared into the darkness and waited for inspiration to hit him over the head. Shit, he knew how to drive a woman wild in bed and out. But he usually took the hands-on approach to foreplay.

He drew a deep breath and began. "Once upon a time, there was a sexy as hell bartender who'd hidden her secret desires for way too long. Sailors, soldiers, and a handful of guys dropped by her bar, chatting and flirting with her. You see, this bartender had long black hair that shone under the bar's dim lights. And every customer who walked through the door noticed the way her jeans hugged her perfect ass. Those men dreamed about touching her, but they knew she'd scare the shit out of them if they tried. This bartender could take down men twice her size with a single pointed look—"

"Because they knew I wouldn't let them in the door when I was working if they caused trouble," she muttered.

"Hell yeah, they knew," he said, the mental picture of the story that was part fantasy, part reality forming in his mind. "But that didn't stop them from picturing this bartender stripped down."

"You're trying to seduce me by telling me every guy who comes into my bar has wondered what I look like naked?"

"I'm *trying* to tell you a bedtime story. You're interrupting," he said. He paused, waiting for another sharp retort. And... nothing. So he continued, "But these men never stopped to think about her secret fantasies. One day a SEAL walked into the bar, took one look at her, and he knew. He vaulted over the bar, took her by the hand, and led her to the back room. After he barricaded the doors with a table to make damn sure her fantasy didn't turn into a crazy threesome in a Jell-O pit—"

Natalie laughed softly. The sound teased his hard-on and left him wishing she'd slip out of her bed and into his. But first, he had to turn her husky laugh into a needy moan.

"He grabbed a black silk sash from the wall and ordered the bartender to strip. Her clothes hit the floor."

"Jack, there aren't any silk ties in the back room. And I don't have a secret desire—"

"Shh, it's my first time," he said. "Don't rush me. Let me tell the whole story. I was just getting to the good part."

He slid one hand beneath the blanket. He'd pulled on a

pair of boxers when he'd climbed into bed to make her feel comfortable. Now, he slipped his hand under the elastic band and gripped the part of his body that freaking loved the mental picture of Natalie tossing her clothes to the ground.

He heard a soft moan from the other bed and his hand froze. He hoped like hell she'd slipped her hands under the covers, too. "Still with me, Natalie?"

"Sorry," she said. "Please continue."

"When the bartender stood naked, her bare tits—uh, breasts—"

"You can say tits, Jack," she said with a laugh.

He'd say whatever she told him to if it turned her on. Right now, he had his own hand wrapped around his dick. And that wasn't how he wanted this night to end.

"He ordered her to climb up on the steel table," he continued. "The bartender obeyed, reaching her arms overhead. He pulled three more silk ties from the wall and walked over to her. Then he grabbed hold of her ankles and drew her to the table's edge, spreading her legs wide. He moved to the other side, tied the silk around her wrists, and secured the fabric to the table legs. He thought about doing the same with her legs, but he left her free to plant her feet on the table. Or wrap her legs around him."

"Jack," she gasped.

Dammit, he wished he could see her face. Were her cheeks flushed from his words? And where the hell were her hands?

"More?" he asked.

"Yes."

One word. No hesitation. He stared through the dark room, trying to make out more than her outline—and failed. He needed night vision, gear he'd forgotten to pack for his weekend trip to Vegas.

"Please," she added, her voice breathless.

And yeah, he couldn't see the effect of his story, but that

one word was all the encouragement he needed to hear.

"He moved between her legs and debated blindfolding her," he said, his hand moving up and down his dick. His hips lifted off the bed and the frame whined. Or maybe that was her bed? Was she touching herself? Had he taken her to a place where desire overrode everything else?

"Go on," she whispered.

"He didn't blindfold her. He wanted her to watch, her eyes on him as she came. He didn't want her to picture someone else running his hands up her legs and slipping a finger inside her wet heat. He wanted her to watch as he lowered his mouth and licked her clit over and over, his finger moving inside her, driving her closer—"

"Jack," she moaned. And his dick threatened to explode.

"He brought her to the edge," he said, the words pouring out in a rush as he struggled to keep his breathing steady. "Learning what drove her wild, what made her pull at the ties binding her wrists—"

"Oh God, Jack… I can't…" she panted. "I just…can't. Not like that."

He heard a rustling. One glance at her bed and he saw her struggling to toss off the covers. She succeeded, breaking free and running through the dark room—

"Shit, Natalie." He released his dick and sat up. "Be careful."

She disappeared into the bathroom. The slamming door echoed in the motel room.

"Natalie?" he called, swinging his legs out of bed. What the hell? She'd sounded like she was into it.

And then he heard it—a barely audible noise. A moan followed by a soft "oh."

"Natalie." He stood and made his way through the darkness to the bathroom door. He stopped and listened. Another soft cry. "Are you okay?"

"Yes," she said, her voice needy and pretty damn close to a "weird sex noise."

He smiled and let the relief wash over him. "I think you liked my story."

"Oh God, yes," she gasped.

"Tell me more, darlin'." He sank to the floor. Resting his back against the door, he closed his eyes and stroked his hardening dick. "Where are your hands? How does it feel? Tell me more."

Chapter Seven

Where are your hands?

Natalie pressed her back against the door and closed her eyes as she sank to the ground. Where were her hands? She'd slipped one into her sweatpants and under the band of her plain black underwear.

Lying in bed and listening to his words, her underwear hadn't felt like one of the six basic pairs she'd bought on sale at the grocery store. Rubbing up against her as she'd pressed her legs together and fought her body's response to Jack's naughty words, her underwear had felt like a silky high-end creation designed for sex.

Silk.

Her imagination recreated the scene Jack had described — the back room of her bar, the steel table, her arms restrained by silk…

Her finger slipped inside, filling her as her thumb pressed against her begging clit. But it wasn't enough. She wanted so much more. She wanted the mysterious SEAL from the story. Except it wasn't a faceless stranger binding her to the table. It was Jack, holding her down and claiming control.

No!

She swallowed a groan as she withdrew her hand from her wet, needy body. The thought of being tied up—that shouldn't leave her headed for an orgasm. She didn't want that—to give up control. Not to anyone.

"Natalie?" Jack called through the door. "I'm here, darlin'. If you need—"

"Where are *your* hands?" she demanded.

She heard a chuckle followed by movement on the other side of the door. The wooden surface at her back pushed against her. No, she wasn't letting him in—

"I'm right here," he said, and she realized he wasn't coming inside. He was leaning against the door. His position probably mirrored hers, his back to the door, looking out into the dark room. "With my hand around my dick, thinking about the sexy bartender from the story, her legs spread wide on the table."

Oh God, yes.

She could picture his hard, thick length, his hand gliding up over the tip, drawing back down. He would know how fast to move his hand as the story played out in his imagination.

"Take off your pants," he ordered. "Do it, Natalie."

She heard the hard edge to his voice. But she didn't obey commands. She set the rules. No one told her what to do.

"Please," he added.

That one word was all she needed. He wasn't taking control from her. It was still her choice. It was still up to her to decide where they were headed. And she *knew* what she wanted.

She hooked her thumbs in the waistband of her sweatpants, drawing them down and taking her plain black underwear with them. She kicked them aside and waited.

And nothing. She could hear him breathing through the

door. Maybe he was too far lost in the fantasy, seeking release. And she should do the same, closing her eyes and picturing Channing Tatum or some other ripped movie star at her mercy. She didn't need to wait for his instructions.

"Spread your legs," he commanded.

The sound of his voice, those words... She mentally slammed the door on the beautiful movie star she didn't want or need right now. She drew her knees up, planted her feet on the bathroom floor, and heal-toed them further and further apart.

"Are you wet?" he asked.

"Yes," she gasped, moving her hand between her splayed limbs, feeling the slick, very real reminder of how her body responded to Mr. Prince Charming. And maybe here, alone in the motel bathroom, with the locked door between them, she could give in to the need, to the fantasy. "Do you still have your shorts on?" she asked.

"No," he growled. "I'm sitting out here bare-ass naked. And I swear, I'm going to come pretty damn soon. But I want you with me. So tell me, what do you need to get there?"

"Talk to me," she said, running her hand over her belly and between her legs. Her finger circled her clit, teasing and taunting her closer and closer. But she didn't want to go there alone. "What would you do if I let you in?"

"I'd watch," he said.

The door shifted at her back. Was he trying to break in? She'd turned the lock. But he was a SEAL. The cheap motel bolt wouldn't keep him out.

"Jack?" she whispered, slipping two fingers inside. It wasn't enough to fill her, to take her over the edge. She swirled her thumb over her clit, moving in earnest, racing toward the end. "Tell me more."

"I'd fall to my knees between your legs and watch your fingers move." The door shifted again. He was lifting his hips, she realized, thrusting his cock into his own hand. And oh God, that image—

"Jack!" She'd never been closer to begging, and this man wasn't even in the room with her. He wasn't touching her. And dammit, he wasn't inside her.

"I'd memorize every touch, learning what made you wet and what drove you wild," he said. "Because next time, it will be my fingers inside you. Darlin', I'll tie those hardworking hands of yours behind your back, and I swear you will beg—"

"I never beg," she shot back. But the image of her hands tied, her body at his mercy…

Five more seconds and she would be lost. Mind, body, and soul dominated by pleasure.

"Come now," she demanded, fighting for control—of him, of the imaginary scene, of herself.

"Not without you," he growled.

"I'm—" She flicked her clit one last time, closing her eyes, picturing that girl tied up on the bathroom floor, at his mercy, under his control. It wasn't her. It couldn't be her.

Her head hit the door as her hips lifted off the floor, seeking more from her hand. And then she was falling head over heels into an orgasm. And this one had a name.

"Jack," she screamed. "Jack, Jack, Jack!"

Jack pictured her smooth skin as he came. He imagined covering her stomach, her thighs, marking her as his. It was primitive—and so fucking hot.

"Natalie," he groaned.

"Yes?" she said, her voice wavering over the one word.

He took several deep breaths as his pleasure receded, then finally answered her. "Next time, I'll be on the other side of the door," he vowed.

"I dare you to try. You're not going to win the bet. And this—tonight—what happened, it doesn't count."

"No," he said, pushing to his feet. He reached for his boxers and used them to clean himself up. "No, it doesn't."

Being in his bed—or hers—meant bodies touching, lips kissing, him buried inside her. He wasn't going to claim he'd won because she'd touched herself while he told her a story.

He headed over to his rucksack and tossed his used boxers to the ground. Then he reached inside for a new pair. He didn't plan to tell anyone about tonight. Oh, he'd let them know when he won the bet all right. But tonight—with a door between them—did not count as a victory in his book. And as a rule, he didn't share the intimate details of every sexual encounter with his brothers, or his teammates.

And this? It felt more personal than most of his relationships. She'd listened to him, really listened, and that had pushed them both over the edge. He'd never experienced anything like it with anyone else.

Of course, he could count his past relationships on one hand. Two. He'd dated two women for longer than a week. But he'd spent most of that time deployed with his team. And in both cases, the distance proved to be too much.

"Is the light still off?" she called through the door.

"Yeah." His eyes had adjusted to the darkness, allowing him to easily move around the room.

"I need you to climb into your bed and stay there," she ordered. "Let me know when you're there, and I'll come out."

"Natalie—"

"And close your eyes," she said. "I need you to keep your eyes shut tight."

He opened his mouth to object…and closed it. He wasn't the only one shaken by what they'd shared through the bathroom door.

He headed for the bed and followed her instructions as if

they'd come straight from his commanding officer instead of the woman he planned to claim. And when he did claim her, he'd do so on his terms. Hearing her reaction to the scene he'd spelled out tonight, he had a feeling Natalie just might let him claim control.

Chapter Eight

"I need you, Jack."

The black-haired beauty repeated those words over and over as she straddled his legs and wrapped her hands around his dick. Looking him in the eyes, she lowered her mouth, bringing her lips closer and closer—

A hand smacked his arm and Jack opened his eyes quickly, taking in his surroundings. He was riding shotgun in Natalie's car. Outside the window, desert stretched for miles beside the highway. And the 100-pound dog snored in the backseat.

"Did you hear me, sleeping beauty?" Natalie said. "I need you to smuggle Mufasa into my room when we get to the hotel. Use your super SEAL skills."

"Unless you want your dog prepped to jump from a helo or go on a diving mission, I don't think my training will help," he said.

She raised an eyebrow. "You can jump from a helicopter, but you can't get a dog into a hotel?"

"Of course I can get him in. But—"

"Thank you," she said. "We're getting close."

Damn if she wasn't determined to challenge him at every turn. He could find a way to smuggle her dog into the hotel. But he had a feeling she could, too. It didn't take BUD/S training to sneak past hotel security. Unless she had more important things to focus on…

"Decide on the perfect favor for the bachelorette tea party?" he asked.

Earlier, after Natalie had sent him out for coffee and food—clearly ready and willing to take advantage of every opportunity to boss him around—they'd hit the road. Two miles into the drive, while he was busy daydreaming about the take-no-prisoners gleam he'd witnessed in her eyes when she'd ordered him to handle the checkout, she'd started debating the merits of different favors for the tea. He'd tried to wrap his mind around the idea of a bachelorette party in Vegas that involved fine china and civilized conversation instead of strippers. And sometime after that, he'd slipped into a combat nap.

"Chocolate body paint," she said, her voice ringing with triumph. "Nothing else combines my sister's favorite things—chocolate, art, and well, now Cade."

And oh sweet Jesus, why had he fallen asleep? Had he missed an entire speech on the pros and cons of edible sex toys? Because damn, that was one conversation he wanted to have—with her.

"If I can find it. I should have time to shop after the poolside meet and greet," she said, changing lanes and exiting the highway toward Sin City's infamous Strip. "Now tell me about your plan to get Mufasa into the hotel."

"We're going to fast rope down to the helicopter pad on the roof. I don't want to risk landing the bird. And I think your pup can handle it. Right, boy?"

Jack glanced at the backseat. Mufasa lifted his head off his paws and let out a bark.

"Jack," she said. "I'm serious."

"So am I. I'll make it happen," he said. "I promise. Now tell me more about the body paint."

Natalie scanned the Greek god inspired pools. Columns, fountains—the setting for her sister's wedding weekend meet and greet was like the adult Disney version of antiquity. A long, narrow pool ran through the center of the space. Smaller, circular pools stood at each end and featured an enormous fountain in the middle.

She studied every statue as she walked by on her way to the cabana reserved for her sister's party. Dionysus. Dionysus. And oh look, another statue of the drunken party god. There were almost as many replicas of the Greek god as there were bars.

She paused on the other side of the narrow, central pool from the cabana and watched the other guests talking. She spotted Lucia in a black one-piece suit. The 1950s style complemented her sister's curves. Two women—a tall, willowy blonde and a plump brunette—chatted with her. Lucia's coworkers from the hospital. Natalie had met them once but had already forgotten their names. She'd have to ask before the bachelorette tea party.

How did I end up here, the maid of honor in Lucia's Vegas wedding to my best friend?

She'd been looking out for her little sister for as long as she could remember. When their parents had died, she'd shouldered her grief and Lucia's. She'd tried to look out for her sister when Lucia announced her plan to pick up a man in Vegas for one wild night. Natalie had sent Cade. And now she was here, ready and willing to celebrate the beginning of her sister's happily ever after.

But the closest I will ever get to a fairy tale ending is a dirty-talking SEAL on the other side of the bathroom door.

Jealousy threatened, but she pushed it away. Lucia deserved a happy ending after everything she had suffered. Still, she couldn't escape the hollow loneliness that bubbled up in sharp contrast to Lucia's bride-to-be glow. Just like she couldn't ignore the fact that for a fleeting moment last night she'd felt connected to someone too—the man on the other side of the bathroom door.

She shoved that thought aside and focused on why she'd endured the disastrous road trip in the first place.

"I can do this. I can be a damn good maid of honor," she whispered as she stared at the fountains and ran through her mental wedding weekend checklist.

1) Buy chocolate body paint

2) Wear the world's ugliest pink dress while my best friend marries my sister

3) Have sex

Before last night, the third item on her to-do list would have ranked below *take on extra shifts at the bar* and *go to the dentist*. But the fact that she'd experienced her first orgasm in mixed company since—crap, she couldn't remember the last nameless face from sixteen months ago. Whoever Mr. Last Time was, he couldn't compete with listening to Jack describe a fantasy. Not Jack's touch. Or his cock—

Across the pool, by the columns leading to the cabana, Jack turned away from Cade and Ronan. He looked right at her and smiled. She was tempted to smile back. Instead, she bit her lip and offered a scowl. He raised an eyebrow. His handsome features, perfect for this godlike setting, seemingly lit with amusement.

This man…

He could make her laugh, make her cry out with pleasure, make her crazy—and he could destroy her controlled life.

And he turned her on. That's why "have sex"—with someone *other* than Jack—had moved up her to-do list. She needed to find someone else to drive her wild for a few hours and erase the physical need. And it wouldn't be Jack. She wanted a man she could control, who wouldn't lead her straight to wild and passionate. A man she could add to the relatively short list of Mr. Last Times and then forget about in the morning.

If she'd learned anything from their impromptu stay at the motel, it was that Jack Barnes was not that man. She'd been fighting to escape the memory of what they'd done, how he'd made her feel as she'd sat on the bathroom floor screaming his name—connected, wanted, desired. Dammit, she'd felt closer to him than the last man she'd slept with and quickly forgotten. And Jack had inspired that connection despite them coming on different sides of the bathroom door.

Lucia stopped by her side, having left her coworkers chatting with a man Natalie didn't recognize. "Most women smile, maybe drool a little, when they see a team of shirtless SEALs by a Vegas pool." Her little sister shoved a drink into her hand.

"I know," Natalie said and accepted the beer. Lucia had to know Natalie would hate the fruity umbrella drink her sister had designated her "signature cocktail" for the long weekend. "I've seen it happen."

Back in Coronado, Natalie had on occasion visited the beach with Cade. She'd grown accustomed to the wide-eyed stares. A hard-bodied Navy SEAL in board shorts, his muscular chest tanned to perfection, drew longing looks, especially from the bikini-clad population. And sometimes Jack tagged along. She'd seen him without a shirt, his suit riding low on his hips. But she'd never wondered about the hard length hiding behind his shorts.

Until today.

Every time he walked past her, greeting friends and teammates, her gaze drifted south. She'd felt his cock through his clothes. And last night, she'd listened as he'd stroked himself. But she'd never seen him naked—

"It was horrible, wasn't it?" Lucia asked. "The drive. With Jack. I'm so sorry you were delayed overnight, stuck with him. I know you two don't get along."

"It was fine," Natalie said firmly.

"You're staring at him as if you can't decide if you should order a hit or do it yourself," Lucia said. "I could have Cade talk to him—"

"No." She didn't need Jack spilling the down and dirty details of what happened last night to her friend. Though she trusted Cade to shut Jack down the minute the conversation crossed the line. Her best friend had zero interest in hearing a play-by-play when it came to Natalie's sex life. Cade respected the fact that she was a big girl capable of handling herself.

"I know Jack has a crush on you," Lucia said.

Natalie raised an eyebrow. "We're not in high school anymore."

And "crush" doesn't begin to describe Chief Jack Barnes' wicked fantasies.

"Call it whatever you want," Lucia said with a wave of her hand. "He wants you in his bed."

Because he bet his brothers and teammates he would sleep with me.

Natalie bit her lip. She wanted her sister focused on the wedding, not Jack's stupidity.

"He can try all he wants. It's not going to happen."

"If you need any help thwarting his attempts—"

"No. You're getting married on Saturday. I know I haven't done the best job of being your sister." Natalie turned and looked at Lucia's damaged face. Red scars ran across her right cheek. If Natalie had been home that night, maybe their drunken foster father would have taken his anger out on her instead of her sixteen-year-old sister. Lucia had been the sweet one, the child eager to fit in with their new families. And then there'd been Natalie, who'd given each new family a hard time, rebelling against the control virtual strangers exercised over her life.

"You're improving," Lucia teased. "And I've forgiven you for sending Cade to watch over me."

Natalie arched an eyebrow. "I have a pink atrocity in my hotel room that makes me wonder. But if you want me to wear the Terrible Tutu I'll do it. I'm here for you. It's your job to enjoy all the parties and get ready for your big day. Don't worry about me. I have a plan for handling Jack."

She could win this bet without her sister or her best friend rushing to her aid. She'd bring Jack to his knees—maybe she'd even tie him up—and then walk away. If she could push him to the point that he was willing to jerk off on the other side of the bathroom door, she could easily drive him out of his mind with a series of Sin City dares.

He thought a bedtime story would break down her defenses? She'd trump that. Before Lucia walked down the aisle, Jack would be ready to admit defeat. He'd wave the white flag of surrender and walk away.

And maybe in the process, she'd steal a glimpse at his cock and lock the image away in her mind. Anything more—a touch, a taste—from the charmer who fantasized about black silk ties was impossible.

"What's your plan?" Lucia pulled free from her arm. "I love you. But Jack is one of the guys looking out for Cade when he's deployed. Please don't piss him off too much."

"I won't." She scanned the pool area. A crescent-shaped pool stood at the far end. In the center, another large fountain shaded the swim-up blackjack tables. Perfect. "I'm just going to challenge him to a little friendly competition."

Chapter Nine

When he walked into the pool area—scratch that, there were *five* pools, including a topless one—Jack thought he'd stumbled upon a smallest bikini competition. Though the winner was probably at the bare breasts pool. Dante, who was finally crawling out from under a rock named Divorce, offered Cade a quick slap on the back before disappearing behind the trees separating the topless area from the other pools. Jack was tempted to join him, but the only tits he wished to see were covered in a black and white polka dot bikini.

Natalie must have missed the itsy-bitsy bikini memo, because hers looked like something women wore in the fifties. Her suit matched Lucia's in style, but Natalie's two-piece revealed a strip of skin beneath her breasts. He'd seen more of her tits when she'd leaned over to kiss him at the bar.

And yet he couldn't take his eyes off her. She was all the more irresistible for how the little bits of her that were visible set his imagination on fire picturing the parts he couldn't see.

Cade, Ronan, and Calvin Daniels, the father of the groom and a retired SEAL, were trading stories. Technically, Jack was part of the conversation. He nodded occasionally and sipped his beer.

"What happened last night?" Cade demanded the moment his father took a break from telling stories about his years with the teams to grab another drink.

"Aww, did you miss me?" Jack teased.

"We were pining for you," Cade deadpanned. "Lucia said you stopped at a motel."

Ronan's eyebrows shot up. "There's no fucking way you won. I'm betting Natalie made you sleep in the car."

"We hit traffic, so yeah, we stopped," Jack said. "But I didn't win the bet."

"Something happened," Cade said. "Look at her. You've received a warmer welcome from our damn targets."

"It's a good thing Natalie doesn't have an AK-47 right now," Ronan agreed. "But if looks could kill, I would be taking your place beside Cade on Saturday."

"She doesn't need a weapon," Jack said. The feisty bartender had more defenses than anyone he'd ever met. When he'd brought up her parents, she'd distanced herself. If she'd had the materials, she would have built a physical wall between them. And then when his story had left her feeling too much, she'd added a barrier to the equation—the bathroom door.

"Between her ice queen stare," Ronan said, "and that mouth of hers—"

"Shut up," Jack said, his voice firm. Ronan outranked Jack. While deployed, Jack wouldn't dare tell an officer to shove it. But Sin City wasn't that kind of hot zone. One more word about Natalie might make Jack snap. And Cade probably wouldn't appreciate a brawl at the first event of his wedding weekend. Speaking of Cade...

"She's your friend," Jack said, turning to the groom. "Why don't you stand up for her?"

Cade cocked his head and kept his gaze focused on Jack.

"Natalie can fight her own battles."

"Doesn't mean you should let Irish here talk shit about—"

Her mouth. The full lips that had kissed him like she wanted to devour him. Shit, imagine what they'd feel like wrapped around his—

"About what?" Cade asked mildly.

"Jesus, it was a joke," Ronan said, shaking his head. "I'm grabbing another drink. Want one?"

"I'm good," Cade said. "But we're keeping the bar open another hour, so have at it."

"I should take advantage of that open bar too," Jack said.

"Look." Cade's gaze met his, stopping him from following Ronan. "I don't want anything to do with your bet. But I know you care about her, and this isn't going to end well."

"She's beautiful. And yeah, I want to win. But I'm not planning a long-term thing." He didn't have a clue how to turn a night, maybe a week, into a relationship. He was willing to give it a shot at some point. But he'd need a helluva lot more than charm to keep something going while he was on the other side of the world for months at a time. That took trust. And he had to face facts. He wasn't good at trusting anyone—or convincing them to trust him—unless it was in the bedroom or on the battlefield.

The women he met at Bottom's Up saw his smile and stopped listening to his words. When his charming face deployed along with the rest of him, so did their interest. He had two failed relationships to prove his theory. And Natalie—she didn't even pretend to trust his smile.

"You care," Cade said firmly.

"Yeah, I do." Jack lifted his beer to his lips and turned his attention to the woman in the black and white bikini. He watched as Lucia moved to Natalie's side. The visible reminder that someone had taken a knife to Cade's fiancée was impossible to ignore in the bright sunlight. Shit, Lucia wasn't even his, but he wished like hell he could erase her pain.

And he had a feeling Natalie did, too.

"Cade, does Natalie ever talk about what happened? To Lucia?"

"No."

"Does she ever say anything about her parents' accident?" Jack asked.

His teammate's brow furrowed. "Not much. I know Natalie holds a grudge against the past."

That makes two of us.

Jack drained the rest of his beer.

"Why?" Cade asked.

"We saw an accident on the road yesterday," Jack explained. "It spooked her."

"And you asked her about it?"

Jack nodded.

"Shit," Cade cursed softly. "If you push her on that, she'll push back. Natalie doesn't open up and let people in. And we're talking about the same woman who made a deal with me to keep you from tossing stupid pick-up lines at her night after night."

"Yeah, she made it pretty clear she hates my lines." Because unlike the other women he'd met in her bar, Natalie actually listened to him. And now she was headed straight for him—or Cade, the man she counted as a friend.

"Stop using them," Cade said.

"That's your advice?" Jack didn't turn to his teammate. He kept his gaze fixed on Natalie as she walked around the pool and came in their direction. The sway of her slim hips, her determined stride—she might not have the smallest bikini, but damn if she wasn't the sexiest woman at the Greek god's poolside oasis.

"I'm not giving you advice on how to talk my best friend into your bed," Cade said, then turned his attention to Natalie as she got within speaking distance. He held out an arm and drew her into his side. "Glad you made it."

She rose on her tiptoes and kissed Cade's cheek. "Mufasa's here and he'd love to see you later."

"I'll smuggle him out for a walk around five," Cade said. He nodded in Jack's direction. "I heard our friend here wrapped our pup in towels and carried him. He pretended our dog was a child."

She turned to Jack, providing an up-close view of the swimsuit that threatened to shred his nerves. "Easier than dropping out of a helicopter?"

"I don't know about that," Jack drawled. "Mufasa isn't exactly light."

"Cade, it's a good thing you're taking him out next. But if you don't want to carry him, I'd suggest borrowing one of the large linen bins by the catering area at the end of my hall," she said as she held out her room key to her friend. "May I borrow the best man?"

"He's all yours." Cade accepted the key and released his hold on Natalie. "But try to bring him back in one piece."

"A SEAL should be able to keep his head above water at the swim-up blackjack tables." She turned and started walking toward the pool that featured tables smack in the center.

"You want to gamble with me?" Jack called after her.

Natalie stopped and glanced over her shoulder. "Oh, yes."

Those lips, that smile…

He'd risk a helluva lot to keep her looking at him just like that while she was on her knees, her mouth ready and willing to take him—

"There's a ten dollar minimum," she said. "First one to double their money wins."

She'd set the limit at twenty bucks. Oh, she was willing to play. But she sure as hell wasn't putting it all on the line. Not yet.

"What's the prize?" he asked.

"If I win, you'll spend the rest of the afternoon running errands with me. I need to pick up the body paint favors for the party and a few other things. You can carry the shopping bags."

Beside him, Cade shook his head and headed for the cabana. If his teammate mumbled a good-bye, Jack didn't hear it. His world had narrowed down to three little words. Chocolate. Body. Paint.

Yeah, he paid attention when she talked, remembering every damn word of their earlier conversation. And body paint? That sounded like his kind of shopping. He was willing to carry the bags straight up to her hotel room.

"I'm game," he said. "But if I win, you'll join me for a swim at the topless pool. And you leave your top behind."

"Deal," she said. "But I won't lose."

"Me neither, darlin'." He walked past her and stepped into the blackjack pool. Win or lose, he had a shot at claiming Natalie before dinner tonight—topless or covered in chocolate.

The sweet taste of victory was within reach. Natalie counted her chips. She'd won the first two hands, but she was still shy of the twenty-dollar mark.

One more hand—maybe two—and then I'll swim away from here the winner.

Of course, Jack might get lucky. If dealt the right cards, he could steal away her win. And that wouldn't accomplish her goal—Jack holding her shopping bags, bored to tears.

But if she added a little distraction… She pursed her lips. Jack understood the basics of blackjack. Still, watching him play the last two hands, she had a feeling he was out of practice. It wouldn't take much to make him forget all about the magical number twenty-one.

She allowed her left foot to drift through the warm water and brush up against his calf. His eyes widened at the unexpected touch but stayed focused on his cards.

"How did you learn to play?" Jack asked, glancing over at her.

"One of my Thursday afternoon regulars." She rocked her hips back and forth. The movement was slow and subtle, but it worked. Her opponent appeared to have forgotten about the cards in his hand.

His brow furrowed. "Which regular?"

Or maybe he was following the conversation, not the way the water lapped at her waist while she moved.

"Jonathan," she said. "He's a former SEAL who was injured in Iraq. He comes in most weeks and we play cards if it is quiet."

"Johnny Smith?" Jack frowned and she abandoned the rocking. "The guy who received a silver star for saving half his team after he'd been shot?"

Natalie nodded and focused on her cards as her foot ran up and down his calf. She signaled the dealer for another.

"Didn't you date him a while back?" Jack asked.

"He asked me to dinner once or twice, but I said no." She glanced up at him, drawing her foot away. "I don't date my customers."

The blonde who'd mistaken the blackjack tables for a wet T-shirt contest leaned over from her stool at Natalie's right. She glanced at the other woman. Now that was a distraction. But why would anyone bother wearing a white tank top into the pool? The see-through fabric clung to the woman's mostly bare breasts. The blonde's bikini top resembled pasties, barely covering her nipples.

"You should try making him jealous if you want his attention," the blonde said in a stage whisper. Natalie would bet all of her chips that the people at the neighboring table could hear her too. "Mack does it to me all the time, and I always fall for it. Afterward the sex is *amazing*."

"Who's Mack?" Natalie had tended bar long enough to know that the best strategy was to steer the conversation away from her personal life and back to Ms. Wet T-shirt.

"My boyfriend." The blonde nodded toward a large, bald man by the bar. "He's getting our drinks and then he'll be right over. You can flirt with him if you want. To make your boyfriend jealous. I promise it will work better than footsy."

"He's not my boyfriend," Natalie said—loud enough for Jack to hear her—and turned her attention to the game. "And I don't flirt."

Jack leaned forward and looked at the blonde. Out of the corner of her eye, Natalie saw his gaze drop to the blonde's most distracting asset—but only for a second. "She means that," he said. "'Go away' is her default response when a guy approaches her."

"And you like that?" The other woman appeared shocked as she signaled the dealer for yet another card. Someone— maybe Mack-by-the-bar—should drag her away from the table before she lost too much.

"Yeah, I do," Jack said. "I know she has her reasons. And one day I'm hoping that she'll let me in and share them with me."

"Don't count on it," Natalie said as she counted her chips. She'd gone over twenty dollars. She'd won. Thank you God. "I don't like to share."

"Darlin', when it comes to you, I don't count on anything," he drawled. "But I don't give up easily."

"Maybe you should have." She pointed to her chips. "Probably would have kept more dignity than outright losing to me." She smiled. "Time to go, Jack." She slid off her stool, taking her pile of chips. "We have a long afternoon of shopping ahead of us."

"Have fun," the blonde called. "And don't forget. Make. Him. Jealous."

"Ma'am." Jack flashed his charming smile at Mack's girlfriend. "Right now, I'm so jealous of an injured hero who had the privilege of teaching her to play cards that I can barely think straight. The footsy was just a bonus."

Natalie frowned as she reached the steps leading to the pool deck. Barely think straight? What had *that* meant? If one conversation could throw Jack's concentration, it was a miracle he'd survived his first deployment with the SEALs.

"That was almost too easy," she murmured as the water splashed at her waist. "Almost like you didn't want to win."

He stood on the other side of the metal handrail, one foot on the bottom step. "Are you suggesting I threw the game?" he asked.

"I think you were pretending to be distracted by our conversation. The blonde in the bikini top…that's another story." She climbed out of the pool, selected a dry towel from the poolside stack, and headed for the lounge chair where she'd left her cover-up. Out of the corner of her eye, she watched Jack run a towel over his dripping wet pecs, his sculpted six-pack…

Jack moved to her side and dropped his towel on the chair. She shifted her gaze away from his muscles and noted the stiff, halted way he grabbed his dry shirt from the chair and pulled it over his head.

He turned to her, and she realized she was clutching to her chest the oversize T-shirt she'd used in place of a fancy beach cover-up. He reached out and placed one finger under her chin, then tilted her head up until she was staring into his blue eyes.

"You're right, I don't get distracted," he said, his tone low and serious. "And I don't give a damn how small that woman's bikini top was. The only tits, shit—the only *breasts* I want—"

"You can say tits, Jack."

He looked hard at her. "The only breasts, the only tits—the only *anything*—I want to see are yours."

The way he looked at her—he wasn't smiling. He always offered a hint of charm with his words. Maybe he turned serious like this on missions with his team, but—

"And I don't cheat, Natalie. I'm not like my brothers. I played the cards I was dealt, plain and simple. Your tricks and that woman's breasts had nothing to do with my loss. Understood?"

"Yes."

He dropped his hand and turned to the cabana. A few of the guests still lingered out front. "I'm going to change into dry shorts," he added. "Then we'll shop."

She'd hit a nerve. There was a lot she didn't know about Jack Barnes. But she had a feeling that his past cut deeper than she'd first suspected.

"I'm sorry, Jack," she whispered as she picked up her bag and headed for the women's bathroom.

Inside, she quickly swapped her wet suit for dry panties, shorts, and an oversize green T-shirt. One glance in the bathroom mirror and she knew she looked like a ragamuffin compared to the well-groomed women in their itty-bitty bikinis. What kind of man would choose shopping with her over a pool filled with beautiful women?

One hell-bent on winning the bet against his brothers.

Or—

One who looks at me and likes what he sees. Who honestly wants me.

God. She wasn't sure which one would be the bigger problem, but she knew which one she wanted and, thus, which one she was desperate to avoid.

"This better be about your brothers, Jack," she said as she left the bathroom. "Because you can't have me."

Chapter Ten

Bang the bartender yet, shrimp?

Jack scanned Colton's text message and debated tossing his cell phone into the pool. He should have walked away from the bet the second the words crossed Colton's lips. He should have said *I want her too damn much to pretend this is just about beating you, jackass.*

The minute he'd said yes to his brother's challenge, Jack had admitted the past still had power over him. And yeah, maybe it gave him an excuse to spend time with the woman who'd held the spotlight in his fantasies for years. But it had also left her wondering if he'd choose a pair of big tits over her. He'd seen the question in her eyes—without the bet, would he try to talk the blonde into a trip to the topless pool to make her boyfriend jealous?

Maybe last week he would have done just that. Though he'd probably have hit on the dealer, not the drunk woman with the x-large boyfriend. But now that he had a chance to get to know Natalie? The woman wasn't just in his fantasies.

She *was* his fantasy, and any other woman would be a distant second trying to match the satisfaction he'd experience finally feeling Natalie's body against his. Another one-night fling with someone who didn't give a damn about him wouldn't do anything for him now. He'd rather have the woman who listened closely, who called him on his shit, and who stood up for him when his brothers reminded him of just how much the past still hurt.

Jack looked down at his phone and started to type. He was tempted to call the whole thing off. But dammit, he couldn't give up. And he sure as shit couldn't hand Colton a victory.

You'll know when I win.

Natalie walked out of the bathroom and spotted Jack standing in front of the cabana. His flip-flop-clad feet were planted hips distance apart, and he'd shoved his hands into the pockets of his tan cargo shorts. At first glance, he appeared relaxed. But the muscles in his jaw remained tight. Where was his smile?

She moved to his side. "Let's go. We have a lot of shopping to do before tonight's dinner."

He gave a curt nod and fell in step beside her. As they exited the pool and headed for the labyrinth of shops located in their hotel, she turned to him. "How bad was it?" she asked. "Growing up with your brothers."

His lips formed a thin line. "By the time I was born, Patrick, the youngest of the bunch, was already seven. I was a surprise. And the rest of them were close in age. My mother called them her 'gang of little men.' They took that to heart. And Colton was their ringleader."

"He's mean," Natalie said as they breezed past the designer stores in search of more affordable shopping.

"Yeah," Jack said, easily keeping pace with her. "I think he had a rough time of it in school. He was always a big guy. He played football, but he was never a starter. I think the popular kids made fun of him."

"So he turned around and picked on you," she said.

Jack nodded. "At first I couldn't take it. I was too little. I ran crying to my mother, which only made it worse. But as I got older, I toughened up and fought back. It wasn't long before I was faster. And it sure as shit didn't take much to outsmart Colton. But sometimes—"

"He cheated," she said.

"Yeah. And not just when we were fighting. His football coach benched him for playing dirty."

"So you decided you'd really show him. You'd become a Navy SEAL. The closest thing to a living, breathing superhero." She stopped at a store window lined with shoes.

He raised his arm and rubbed the back of his neck. "Not many people know this," he said, lifting his gaze from the floor. He looked at her from beneath his long lashes. "My mom was always reading romance novels. She'd hide them in the kitchen, pulling the paperbacks out to read a few pages while she waited for dinner to finish up in the oven. One time, when I ran to her in tears—I was still young, maybe six or seven—she told me about this character. He'd been a shrimp like me, the skinny kid who got picked on. But he defied the odds and became a Navy SEAL. After that day, I became obsessed with the SEAL teams. I learned everything I could and swore I'd do whatever it took to be one."

Her eyes widened and her lips formed a smile. "You joined the SEALs to become a romance hero?"

"No, I joined to serve my country and prove to my brothers I could do anything I put my mind to," he said, lowering his arm and placing both hands on his hips. His stance mirrored hers—challenging, ready to launch into battle. "Anything."

Including her. He didn't need to say the words. The bet hung in the air between them. She'd let her heart melt a little for the bullied boy pushed around by his brothers, but she wasn't about to wave the white flag and surrender.

"You lost this round, Jack. Now it's time to shop." She dropped her hands to her sides and headed for the shoe store.

"Wait." He wrapped fingers around her arm, drawing her back. And she couldn't blame him. She wasn't looking forward to picking out a pair of heels.

She pulled her arm free. "You lost the dare—"

"I know," he said. "But I thought we were hunting for chocolate body paint."

"That's on the list." She led the way into the store and headed to the section marked sale. "But first, I need to find a pair of heels to wear with my bridesmaid dress."

If he could survive lying in position for twenty-four hours hidden from sight, waiting for a go from his commanding officer, he could manage shoe shopping. But could Natalie?

She stared at the display tables as if they were littered with live explosives. She picked up a strappy silver sandal with a low heel. "What do you think?"

"Looks great," he said.

Please let her buy the first pair she sees.

A saleswoman appeared at Natalie's side. "Can I help you?" She looked to be about twenty years his senior and either highly caffeinated or seriously into her job. "Oh, I love those sandals. And they're twenty percent off. But we only have them in a size five."

"I'm a seven," Natalie said flatly as she placed the shoe back on the display table. "I'm looking for something that will match a pink bridesmaid dress designed for an insane ballerina. The dress stops at my ankle, or close to it. And something on sale would be best."

The saleswoman blinked and then nodded. She walked over to the wall and picked up a high-heeled, shiny sandal with an intricate pattern. A zipper ran up the back. "These aren't on sale, but they're priced about the same as some of the marked down shoes. They're also comfortable. Would you like to try them on?"

"Yes," Natalie said quickly. She sounded eager to have their visit to the land of shoes end as soon as possible. She sat down on the leather bench as the saleswoman disappeared into the back.

Jack claimed the space beside her, leaning forward and resting his forearms on his thighs. "You know, I never would have intentionally lost"—hell, he couldn't even say the word cheated—"to end up here."

"I know," she said, accepting the box from the saleswoman with a nod. "But I also know you want to win."

He watched as she unceremoniously pulled the heels from the box. She kicked off her sandals and then slipped the new shoes on.

"They fit," she announced. One glance at her impartial expression and he had a feeling that when it came to footwear, her excitement matched his—which was zero. He didn't give a damn what she wore on her feet. He wasn't drawn to her shoes, or, shit, her clothes. It was the woman beneath—the soft curves and the fiery, touch-me-if-you-dare attitude—that left him wanting to do a helluva lot more than watch her try on heels.

"Why are you fighting me?" he asked Natalie when the saleswoman left them and carried the box toward the cashier. "Last night—"

"I'm not right for you," she said, standing up.

"After watching you shop for shoes, I think you're wrong."

He followed her to the register. He waited until she'd paid the saleswoman and accepted her purchase.

"Just because we both dislike shoe shopping doesn't make us a perfect match," Natalie said drily.

No, but it was one more checkbox on his mental list of things he liked about her. Once they were outside the store, he spoke up. "The way you screamed my name through the bathroom door, I got the impression that you wanted me, too."

"I'm not interested in black silk ties." She thrust the shopping bag into his hands.

"It was just part of the story."

"It doesn't work for me," she said firmly.

Bullshit.

He'd heard her come. She'd liked the fantasy he'd described.

"Plus, we argue," she said.

Because she actually listened to him—every stupid line, every dumbass remark, and every piece of his past.

"Not about things that matter," he said.

"You just want to win—"

"I do," he admitted. "But I also want you, Natalie. And I have a feeling you want me, too." He watched as her gaze drifted lower and stopped at his crotch. "Another story. Only this time, we stay on the same side of the door. Nothing between us."

She looked up at him, her brown eyes staring into his. Lips parted, the same question—fight or flight—that he saw in her expression night after night from the other side of the bar. And he'd never seen her run. From anything. "Jack—"

He closed the space between them and placed his finger over her lips. He wouldn't let her run from her own desires, not this time. "I dare you to let me prove it," he murmured. "Prove you're dying to get into my pants as much as I want into yours."

She pushed his hand away. "We're not done shopping yet."

"After we buy the favors, I dare you to come to my room and test the paint." Her eyes widened at the word *dare*, and he knew he had her. She wouldn't walk away from a challenge.

"And once I've licked every bit of chocolate off of you," he continued, "I challenge you to walk away from this. From us."

She placed her hands on her hips, her gaze locked with his. Her dark eyes burned bright with determination.

"Accepted." Her eyes narrowed. "But I bet the chocolate tastes just as good on you."

"I'm counting on that." He took her hand and led her through the mall.

"And you'd better be ready," she said. "Because I *am* walking away."

He pulled her through the crowd, bypassing designer stores and packed restaurants. "Darlin', when I finish licking you, I promise you'll feel too good to head for the door. Maybe in the past that worked for you—"

"I haven't—" She pressed her lips closed, holding back the rest of that sentence.

He raised an eyebrow but didn't say a word as they kept walking. A few stores down, they stopped in front of a shop with a window displaying pictures of women lost in pleasure. Oh hell yeah, he wanted to see Natalie's expression when the big O hit her—with or without the aid of the adult toys hidden behind the banner.

"This is it," she said at the same time he said, "This looks like the right place."

He marched into the sex toy store with Natalie at his heels. He walked past the dildos and whips. With a cursory glance at the handcuffs, he scanned the space and located a sales clerk.

"We need a half dozen bottles of chocolate flavored body paint." He glanced at Natalie, who stood by his side, every inch of her petite form pulsing with a battle-ready energy. "Will that be enough? Or do you need more?"

She looked down at his crotch again. Jesus, if she kept doing that, he'd toss her over his shoulder and flat-out run for his room. But she let her gaze linger, not giving a damn that the sales clerk was watching and waiting.

"More," she said. "I'm hoping I'll need a lot more."

Chapter Eleven

"Jack, this room…"

Natalie dropped the Sizzling Secrets shopping bag on the floor of the *marble entryway*. Her deluxe queen bedroom could fit in the sitting area. Her gaze swept over the loveseat nestled between two armchairs. A minibar completed the sitting area. And the bed—oh wow, the king-sized, four-poster bed beckoned like—

"It's like a fairytale," she murmured.

"I upgraded."

"And they just happened to have the biggest suite available when you checked in?"

"Cade has the largest," he said, and she raised an eyebrow. "Room," he added. "Cade booked the largest suite. And I thought what the hell? I still own a portion of the family cattle ranch and it's been doing well, so why not?"

Oh yes, someone lied about needing to share a room that first night in middle of nowhere California.

Or maybe Cade had clued Jack in on Natalie's shoestring budget. But she didn't want pity from Jack.

He bent down and plucked the chocolate body paint from the bag.

Or chocolate covered orgasms. She didn't want those either.

Now who's the liar?

He kept his gaze on her as he unscrewed the top and tossed it to the floor. "I have a story for you, and this one comes with a happy ending."

He dipped his fingers into the paint.

Take charge!

Her brain fired the command, but her limbs refused to move. She glanced at the bed. She had a plan, dammit. And it did not involve a four-poster frame fit for a queen.

"Once upon a time, there was a warrior princess," he began, "who challenged a prince to a chocolate-covered orgasm duel."

She laughed and shook her head. "A duel with a *man*," she corrected. He might be the Prince Charming of the Navy SEALs, but in here, with her, he was just Jack. If she lost sight of that…heaven help her, he might win. "A man destined to lose the duel."

"Take off your shirt, princess."

The deep rumble of his voice seemingly bypassed her common sense, speaking directly to her hands. Her fingers toyed with the edge of her T-shirt. And then he smiled at her. A sweet, playful, and—dammit—reassuring grin.

Oh God, this time I might hand over my panties.

She pulled her T-shirt over her head and tossed it aside. She squared her shoulders and faced him wearing only her bikini top and jean shorts.

"Place your hands behind your head," he ordered as he dipped his finger into the chocolate. He reached forward and painted a line over the swell of her breast, careful to avoid her suit. His touch sent a shiver down her spine.

"Jack," she said, her voice soft and needy.

He looked her straight in the eyes. "Yes?"

"I want to touch you."

"Believe me, I want that, too." He drew a line over her other breast. The chocolate felt warm on her skin. And the anticipation—waiting for him to lick it off—left her body aching to be painted, touched, and tasted.

"But right now," he continued, "I need you to place your hands behind your head."

She curled her fingers against her palms, forming tight fists at her sides. "I can't. If I let you win—"

"Natalie." His tone was gentle but still sparked with desire. "This isn't about the bet. We won't touch the bed. This is just me wanting you. Like crazy. For so damn long."

She swallowed, then murmured, "How long?"

"From the first time you told me to sit down, shut up, and drink my beer." He dipped his hand into the chocolate again. Slowly, he connected the lines on her breasts, allowing his finger to dip into her cleavage.

"Would it work now?" she asked. "If I told you to sit down, shut up, and let me paint you?"

He chuckled. "You'll get your turn."

"But—" She closed her eyes as his finger slid beneath the small knot of polka-dot fabric nestled between her breasts. He pulled it forward. And she opened her eyes to see him stealing a peek at her breasts. "I want to go first," she said.

To dominate. To win. To leave you wanting.

"Not a chance, Natalie." His finger brushed the side of her breast. She gasped. Oh God, she wanted to melt into his touch.

"Jack."

"That's it, darlin'," he murmured, his fingers moving up and down the sides of her breasts, teasing, tempting…and then he stopped.

"Jack," she pleaded.

No, no, no! Do not beg.

"Take off your bikini top," he said. "Let me in. Let me see you."

She reached for the closure at her back and released the top. The straps slid off her shoulders, and she tossed the bikini beside her shirt.

"Natalie." He dropped to his knees and set the jar of paint by her feet. Still staring at her bare breasts, he dipped one hand into chocolate and scooped out a handful. "Please place your hands behind your head," he said as he rubbed his palms together.

This time, she obeyed. She raised her arms, pressed her palms against her hair, and interlaced her fingers. The sight of this man at her feet—

He reached up and wrapped his large, powerful hands around her oh-so-average-sized breasts. Leaving behind a pair of handprints, he traced lines over her skin. His thumbs brushed back and forth over her nipples. Sensation rippled through her. She was so close to giving in and letting him claim every inch of her. So close—

He leaned forward, his height offering an advantage even though he was on his knees, and licked the underside of one breast. And she moaned. The sound filled the entryway.

"Tell me," she demanded. "What did you want while you watched me from the other side of the bar?"

"This." His hands moved to the button on her shorts. He left chocolate marks as he freed the closure and drew the zipper down. Then he pulled her shorts down her legs. "Kick them off."

She sent her shorts flying across the room as he dipped his hand into the body paint again. And now she was standing in front of the one man she'd never planned to fall for wearing only her underwear.

"I wanted you." He drew a chocolate line from her chest to the top of her panties. "I wanted a peek behind your defenses." His tongue ran over her skin, licking up the path. When he reached the fabric, he paused.

"My underwear isn't a barricade waiting to be stormed," she said.

He laughed. "Nine times out of ten, you turned your back to me when I came into the bar. And I've been dying to find out if your ass feels as good as it looks."

"Jack." She struggled to add a note of warning to her voice. But he ignored her. His chocolate-covered hands ran up the backs of her thighs and slipped beneath her underwear.

"Perfect," he murmured.

"You wanted to see me naked," she said, staying focused on their sexual connection.

"Yes." He glanced up at her. "And I wished to slip behind the invisible walls you erected the moment I walked in the door. I've dreamed about touching you. But Natalie, I also want to learn more about the fierce woman who appears so damn determined to keep everyone at arm's length. All that fire—it must be protecting something."

"Me," she said softly. She kept the world away, protecting her heart from another loss, another rejection. And another wrong turn that would end in guilt and pain.

"You're safe with me." He leaned forward and drew the top of her underwear away from her stomach with his teeth. His tongue darted out, licking her skin.

"Jack." She arched her back and pressed her hips forward against his lips. She wanted more, so much more, here in the entryway, where it didn't count toward the future. This wasn't about the bet. The way his tongue slid lower and lower beneath her underwear...the feel of his hands cupping her ass...that was all that mattered right now.

He gently released her panties as his hands slid out from

her backside and stripped her naked.

"Step out and spread your legs," he said. "Let me in. Let me taste you."

"You can't possibly…"

"Watch me." He smiled up at her as he slipped one hand between her legs.

"Stop looking at me like that," she gasped. His index finger explored, teasing and testing her. "I already gave you my underwear."

He laughed and slid his finger inside her as his thumb brushed her clit.

"Jack!" she cried, hating the note of desperation in her voice. But she needed him to do something. Her knees threatened to buckle. "It's been so long. And it feels so good. I can't… I'm going to fall."

"I've got you." He abandoned his intimate touch and wrapped his hands around her waist. Then he lowered his head and ran his tongue over her clit. Once. Twice.

And then he pulled away.

"What are you doing?" she demanded. "You can't stop."

"Do you think I can make you come like this? Do you dare me to try?" He bent his head and licked her again, offering just enough pressure to drive her wild—and then… nothing.

"Jack," she said through clenched teeth. "I won't beg."

"I'm not asking you to. I've dreamed about doing this for too damn long to wait," he murmured. One more lick, and oh, the sensations rushing forward, pushing her closer. Then he drew back.

She stared down at the Navy SEAL on his knees, waiting for her answer. "Yes," she said. "I dare you."

His smile faded and his jaw tightened. The look in his blue eyes—it was pure heat. "Watch me, Natalie. And when you come, scream my name."

Keeping his hands wrapped around her hips, he buried his face between her legs and licked his way to her clit. His tongue stroked and teased, then swept lower and slipped inside.

He let out a deep moan and withdrew his tongue, leaving her feeling empty. She wished he would use his hands, fill her with his fingers. But he wouldn't lose the dare.

As if reading her thoughts, his grip tightened around her hips. He licked and sucked. The movements shifted from controlled and measured to wild and erratic. He gave her more and more and more.

She closed her eyes. She couldn't watch the too charming SEAL worship her body with his mouth. But as soon as she shut out the sight of this man, on his knees, his large frame bending at impossible angles, her feelings threatened to overtake the pure bliss.

She'd ridden an emotional roller coaster for years, racing through grief, hostility, and rejection. The ride never stopped. But she'd never reached this peak. The SEAL kneeling at her feet thrust her into unfamiliar territory. She'd dated. She'd slept with men—maybe not recently—but she was always careful to keep them at arm's length. Still, she'd never felt worshipped. She'd never met a man who threatened to push her vibrator into second place when it came to his ability to make…her…

"Jack!" Her hands fell from behind her head. She needed to touch him, feel him. And make damn sure he didn't stop. Her fingers gripped his shoulders, nails clawing at his shirt. "Jack, oh God, Jack!"

His tongue pressed against her clit and she detonated. The pleasure spiraled upward, claiming control of her body, and pushing into her mind. She let go, riding the high until—

It stopped. Natalie opened her eyes and glanced down at the large warrior panting at her feet. His biceps bulged, his muscles working overtime to keep her upright.

"I win," he murmured.

"What?" She fought to collect her thoughts. Her body hummed with the aftershocks of an orgasm that put her vibrator to shame, and he thought he'd won?

"The dare," he reminded her.

She stumbled back, out of his reach, and focused on staying upright. She refused to melt into a puddle in front of him. And she sure as hell wasn't going to leave him feeling like he'd come out on top.

He thought he'd won? No. The battle had only just begun.

She placed her hands on her hips. "Time to hand over your boxers, Jack."

Chapter Twelve

Jack could go from zero to sixty when he received an order. Part of it was training. But right now, desire drove him to pull his T-shirt over his head and toss it aside. He kicked his shoes away as he stripped off his cargo shorts. When it came to getting naked, he generally issued the commands. But he'd heard the tremor in Natalie's voice, and he knew that she needed him to obey.

She'd raised her defenses again. Her walls were up. And if he failed to follow orders—if he failed to show her she was still in control—she might fall apart. Or worse—bolt for the hall. He had a hunch she'd literally slam the door in his face rather than leave her weakness, the one point that made her vulnerable, visible for everyone to see.

She liked him.

And he had a hunch that scared the hell out of her.

So he'd try his best to do as she asked, but—

"Forgot to pack your underwear?" she murmured, her gaze fixed on the one part of his body that desperately wanted to keep her on his side of the door. "You travel so much for work that I figured you had it down."

He laughed. Travel for work? That was one way to look at his deployments to parts of the world most Americans would place dead last on their future vacation wish lists.

"I skipped the boxers—and the briefs—after our swim," he said. "I hope you're not disappointed."

Her gaze met his. While his dick missed being her focal point, he liked the humor he saw in her big brown eyes.

"I'm crushed," she said, her voice heavy with sarcasm. "I was planning to use your boxers as a pillow while I knelt down and took your cock in my mouth."

"How about my shirt? Or a couch cushion? Hell, we could move to the chairs," he said, quickly playing through every alternative. They could skip straight to plan Z as long as it ended with her lips wrapped around him.

"How about this?" Her voice was so damn sexy that his balls drew up, wishing to be closer to her. And yeah, she was clearly on the same page. She bent at the waist and lowered her mouth to his crotch.

"Jesus," he said as she placed her hands on his hips. She wasn't using him for balance despite the fact that her position looked like a picture out of a Blow Jobs for Yoga Instructors book. No, she was holding him in place. Like he would move away from the scene playing out in front of him.

"Place your hands behind your head," she said, her lips close enough to lick the drops of liquid beading at the tip of his dick.

"Yes, ma'am." He'd never uttered those words to a woman on the verge of rocking his world. But staring at the way Natalie's back formed a long line, and shit, the way her legs remained stick straight, thrusting her ass up—he'd do just about anything to keep her here. So he raised his arms and interlaced his fingers behind his head.

"Do you dare me to make you come? To leave you

screaming my name?" she challenged, rising up on her tiptoes as if she'd stepped into a pair of skyscraper heels. And the effect on her ass, thrust higher into the air—

"Yes." He managed the one word through clenched teeth. Because if she didn't take him into her mouth soon…hell, he might explode just from looking at her.

She ran her lips down his length, drawing him deeper and deeper into her mouth. His jaw clenched, but he kept his eyes open, focused on her.

"Seeing you like this," he said, his voice rough. "I want to slide into you from behind. I want to take you right here, bent over the edge of the couch, then over the bed—"

Her tongue pressed against him as her mouth ran up and down, up and down…aw hell, he was on the fucking edge, primed to explode.

"Natalie, I'm dying—" He inhaled sharply, fighting to hold back and make this moment last. "I'm dying to run my fingers through your hair, hold tight to your head, and fuck your sweet mouth."

She released his right hip and wrapped her hand around the base of his dick—a not-so-subtle reminder that she was calling the shots here. She maintained a firm grip on him as she moved her hand up to touch her lips.

"Fuck me," he growled. He settled for pressing his fingers against his own skull, his hands still behind his head.

She owned this moment. And the way she touched him, her hand stroking him while she sucked harder and faster, the way she rocked back and forth on her tiptoes using her entire body to literally blow him away—she knew it.

He closed his eyes and surrendered. He wasn't going to win this one. But shit, if losing felt this good—

"Natalie!" He roared her name. Hips pumping into her mouth, he came so damn hard his knees threatened to give out. But she didn't let him go. The petite woman who'd driven him crazy from across the bar held tight and sucked him dry.

When she released his very grateful dick, he opened his eyes and fought to catch his breath. Jesus, he'd barely moved a muscle and was winded. Natalie stood up straight and placed her hands on her hips.

"I'm sorry," he said. "I should have warned you I was about to come. Give me a few minutes, and darlin', I'll make it up to you."

He glanced at the bed. He wanted her flat on her back, hands above her head, while he pushed into her more than he wanted his next breath. And right now oxygen was pretty damn high on his priority list.

"No," she said firmly. "We're done."

"Natalie." He closed the gap between them and raised his hand to her breast. He brushed the dried chocolate paint off her nipple. One touch and his lower half shifted from *I'm satisfied* to *Give me more*. "This doesn't end like this. Climb onto the bed and let me lick you clean." She still seemed hesitant, but he had an idea how to tempt her. "And when you're wet and ready, I want you to reach your arms up overhead and hold on. Grip the headboard, the sheets, just don't let go until you come."

"No." She pulled away and quickly scooped her clothes off the floor.

"Natalie—"

"I need to leave."

"You're still covered in chocolate," he said, tracking her movements as she pulled on her bikini top. "At least stay for a shower. Let me wash you."

"You won this round, Jack. But you won't win the bet. This won't happen again."

"Let's call this round a tie," he said.

She turned to him, her lips—oh God, those lips—forming a thin line. "A tie?"

"Better yet, let's say this has nothing to do with the bet." He paused. "I'm only asking for a little more time with you."

No dares. No challenges. Not this time. He wanted her to stay because he wanted to be with her a little longer.

"I'm not going to have sex with you in the shower," she said firmly. "Or anywhere else in this room. Not your bed. Not on the couch, or the floor."

"Understood," he said, fighting a smile. The woman who'd just made him come so hard he saw stars was determined to list every location they would not be getting it on if she stayed. And the hell of it was that in this moment, he'd rather be naked with her and not doing anything than doing everything with any other woman. She walked past him and headed for the bathroom. She stopped at the door and glanced back at him. "Are you coming?"

"Affirmative," he said. He knew when to take an order.

She held up her finger. "I mean it. No sex. Not here. Not anywhere."

She turned to go into the bathroom, and his gaze dropped to her perfect ass. He followed her, shaking his head, trying to recall if he'd ever been this excited—and shit, happy—to *not* get laid.

There was no such thing as "just a shower" with a Navy SEAL. She hadn't set foot under the rush of warm water, but she could state that for a fact. When they'd reached the bathroom, she'd turned on the water and stepped away to remove her bikini top. And Jack had slipped into the shower.

He tipped his head back, his biceps on display as he ran his hands through his short, wet hair. Water rushed down his back and over his sculpted chest muscles. In the windowless bathroom, illuminated by the harsh light, he sparkled as if he were something special.

He is, she thought, reaching for the door. But she wasn't looking for that special someone in her life. She'd told herself one taste, one touch. But…

Her gaze ran down his body. Parts of him were pretty damn hard to walk away from. Too bad all of his positives weren't located below the belt.

"You know you need to stand under the water to wash away the chocolate," he said, blinking his eyes open as he stepped out from under the spray.

"I was waiting for you to calm down," she said with a pointed look at his large and very eager cock.

He threw his head back and laughed. "Darlin', I have this reaction every time I walk into Bottom's Up."

"I bet the other bartenders appreciate the greeting," she said, opening the shower's glass door and stepping inside. The space could probably have held his entire team and featured two showerheads mounted on the wall. She stepped under the one turned on and allowed the warm water to strip away the sticky feeling left behind by the chocolate.

"I only stop by the bar when you're working," he said as she closed her eyes.

"You like being ignored that much?" she said, not daring to open her eyes and witness the look accompanying those soft words.

"You're not ignoring me now," he said, his lips brushing her ear.

Damn him, he'd moved behind her and she hadn't even realized it. She blinked open and stepped forward. His hand touched her shoulder, not a firm grip, but enough to stop her from rushing out of the shower stall. She waited for him to press his long, hard length against her backside. And waited…

He released her, and she heard the sound of a bottle opening.

What in the...

Then she felt his hands in her hair and smelled the soothing fragrance of mint-infused shampoo. Just when she thought he was about to disregard her no-sex-in-the-shower ultimatum, he surprised her.

"No, I'm not ignoring you," she murmured, closing her eyes as his hands massaged her scalp.

"And you're only pretending to at the bar," he said.

"Hmm," she murmured, refusing to confirm the truth behind his statement—and because his hands felt oh so good in her hair.

"How did you end up working at Bottom's Up?" he asked.

"I wanted to live near the beach," she said. "Someplace warm. When I arrived, I drove around looking for a job, and Justin, the owner, gave me a shot. I think he felt sorry for me."

"That must have pissed you off."

"Yes," she said with a laugh as he withdrew his hands from her hair. He placed his hands on her shoulders and gently guided her back until she stood under the shower's spray. He rinsed out the shampoo and led her back to the open space, never once pressing up against her and showing her how much he wanted to do more than shampoo her hair. Of course, his interest in more may have died down.

One way to know for sure...

She opened her eyes and glanced down at his cock, still hard and oh so eager to do more than wash her hair. His eyes met hers as she turned to face the wall, and he raised an eyebrow.

"I'm not finished with your hair." He plucked the miniature conditioner bottle supplied by the hotel from a built-in shelf.

"I thought we were just rinsing off the chocolate," she said as his fingers ran over her scalp again. The pleasure of his touch rippled through her, and her breasts begged to be next.

"I don't do anything halfway, darlin'," he murmured.

"The benefits of being bathed by a SEAL."

He laughed, drawing her back for another rinse. "Now that you've proved yourself to Justin and terrified half the soldiers and sailors in Southern California, what's next?"

She stepped forward, her hair clean, and waited for him to wash the rest of her. "I'm content right where I am," she said, hoping to draw the conversation away from the future and back to the lingering bits of chocolate on her skin.

"Life's not as much fun if you stay in one place." He closed the space between them and placed his hands on her breasts. Gently, he began to wash away the body paint.

"I don't dream about a white picket fence and two point five kids," she said sharply despite the wicked, wondrous sensations rushing from her chest down to her toes.

"Me neither. At least not for a while. I want to be there for my kids. Right now, I'm 'travelling for work' too much."

Despite the teasing tone he used to deliver those words, quoting the exact phrase she'd used earlier, a kernel of hope drew her attention away from his touch. "You're planning to leave the teams?"

And start a family?

She mentally chided herself. Was that really the answer she was hoping for from him?

She tried to push away dreams of children. She wasn't in the right place for kids now. And she had a sinking feeling she might never get there. But here, in his shower, hope seemingly rained down on her as though it had been mixed in with the water.

"One day," he said. "I can't be a SEAL forever. Just like I'm guessing you aren't planning to rule over Bottom's Up for the rest of your days."

"Probably not," she said. Still, the hope burned bright

despite her words. Oh yes, there was definitely something in the Sin City water. Or maybe it was simply his touch, his voice, and heaven help her, his questions. Asking about her future, while touching her as if he could worship her breasts for days, like he would happily wash her hair until his balls turned blue just to be near her...

"I could stay here forever," she murmured.

"They might miss you at the bachelorette party tomorrow," he teased. "But I bet we could find a use for the chocolate body paint."

"That wouldn't be fair to Lucia," she said.

"Maybe not. But it would be fun." He released her breasts and ran his hands over her stomach. He reached for her hips and drew her back against him until she could feel one hard, thick reason to stay right here, with him, for a long, long time.

If she didn't have a wedding party buffet to attend tonight, she might have stayed with him until the sunset.

No, I can't do that to Lucia.

She'd have to satisfy herself with moments in-between making small talk at dinner and prepping party favors, seconds where she could fantasize about the look on his face when she'd taken him in her mouth, the thrill when they'd been in the shower and he'd lathered her naked body with soap and a touch that drove her wild—

"I need to go," she said as she stepped forward and broke his hold on her. "I can't skip tonight's dinner. And neither can you."

He glanced down at his revived erection. "Yeah, but I'm going to have a helluva time facing the other guests. Especially if you're in the room."

She smiled. Knowing that he'd be fantasizing about her too—oh yes, that would comfort her as she attended one wedding event after another. Her imagination might take a side trip—or twenty—to revisit this moment, in his shower, with his cock practically begging her to stay.

She pushed out of the glass door and reached for a towel. Behind her the water turned off, but she didn't turn to look at him. She saw now how to bring him to his knees and leave him wanting more. And knew she could win no matter what happened with the bet.

She glanced over her shoulder at the dripping wet sailor tracking her movements, his gaze filled with a mix of amusement and desire. And one look at his lower half confirmed that he still wanted her.

Her opponent was still standing, but she'd won this round.

"This feels good," she said, securing the towel at her breasts and relishing her victory.

He raised an eyebrow. "I can do better than a towel."

She laughed. "Good. Because you're going to need to up your game if you plan to win the next round."

Up my game? Win the next round?

Naked and still dripping, Jack followed Natalie out of the bathroom. She pulled on her clothes with stunning efficiency. But her gloating grin remained firmly in place.

He stole a glance at the untouched bed. He wanted to toss her on the smooth surface and keep her there until they were tangled in the sheets, hot, sweaty, sated, and ready for another shower. He wanted to claim the ultimate victory.

But he could wait. They'd get there. After that shower, he felt pretty damn sure he'd win the bet. Another time. Right now, he wanted to keep that smile on her lips.

He placed his hands on his hips and cocked his head, ready to challenge her. "That was just a shower, Natalie."

She arched an eyebrow. "When was the last time you had a shower like that?"

"Never," he admitted as he closed the space between them.

Her dark eyes dropped to his dick, lingered a moment, and then shifted back to his face. He stopped in front of her. He was close enough to reach out and pull her close, but he didn't dare.

"I played by your rules in the shower," he said, his gaze locked with hers. "No sex. Take away that rule…and trust me darlin', you'd never look at a shower the same way again."

"Maybe not," she said with a wide, daring grin. She stepped back until she bumped into the door. She reached for the knob. "But you won't win."

She opened the door and disappeared into the hall. She moved quickly, seemingly determined to have the last word.

"Yes, I will," he murmured to the empty entryway.

Because he didn't lose. Ever.

And because Cade was right. Jack cared a lot more than he should for the woman who'd made it clear she didn't want him—not in her bed, not in her shower, and not in her life.

Except when he issued a challenge…

Chapter Thirteen

"I hear Jack survived the afternoon," Cade said in his familiar baritone. "How about a drink? I owe you for giving my best man a ride and entertaining him today."

Natalie looked up from the creative seafood display and raised her champagne flute. "Thanks, Cade, but I've already taken a trip to the open bar."

He sighed and crossed his arms in front of his chest. "Determined to hide behind the shrimp all night?"

"I'm not hiding," she lied, which was foolish because a) Cade would call her bluff, and b) she'd won. She'd walked out of Jack's room and left him wanting more. And yes, maybe she should have done that before they'd taste-tested the chocolate body paint. But it had ended up working out for her anyway.

Just knowing she'd been able to step into the shower with him—nothing between them but water and soap—and resist the temptation to jump him, that knowledge sent a wave of confidence through her. She could do this. Hell, she'd done it.

The bad thing was that now, having seen him naked and felt his hands rub her body...

Every time she closed her eyes, she pictured climbing up onto his gigantic hotel bed and stretching her arms overhead. And her imagination didn't stop there. She pictured herself spreading her legs as he knelt between them, ready to sweep her off into the land of sweet dreams and orgasms.

"Natalie?" Her best friend's voice pulled her out of the fantasy. "Are you okay?"

"Fine," she said, refusing to look up at Cade. She couldn't risk him seeing the stoked desire flowing through her.

"You sure? You look a little…flushed."

She laughed, hoping that would mask her feelings. "Just mentally preparing to walk down the aisle looking like a blind and bat-shit crazy ballerina."

"Do you want me to talk to Lucia?" he asked. "I don't know if she can fix the crazy, but there's a chance she'll let you wear another dress."

Natalie shook her head. "No. I owe my sister for sending you to Vegas to babysit her."

And for leaving her alone with our drunken asshat of a foster father because my stupid need to rebel, to claim control of my life, trumped everything.

"If you change your mind, just say the word," Cade said.

"Natalie, there you are," Jack called as he headed over to her.

Great, now she was trapped in the corner, her back to the wall, shrimp in front of her, and a Navy SEAL on either side.

Except she had nothing to be nervous about. Not after that shower. She'd *won*, and Jack coming over here was the perfect opportunity for her to remind him of that fact.

"You look down," she said to Jack. "Something not go according to plan?"

He raised an eyebrow at her and smiled. Yeah, he knew exactly what she was talking about.

"I have something you want," he said.

Her eyes widened. She looked at Cade to keep from stealing a glance below the best man's waistline. Thanks to this afternoon, she knew for a fact that his jeans, her fears, and the fact that he'd win the bet were the only obstacles between her and *what she wanted*. Oh, and the room full of friends and family.

Her best friend's mouth formed a thin line. "I thought you promised," Cade said. "No more one-liners."

Jack laughed. "This time, it's true. She left the bachelorette party favors in my room. I would have brought them down, but I didn't want to reveal the surprise."

Cade glanced at her and raised an eyebrow, but he didn't say a word.

"Leave the bag at the front desk," she said. "I'll grab it later."

"Sure you want to pick up a giant plastic bag from a sex toy shop from the bellhop?" Jack challenged. "I could bring it by your room later."

"No, I'm—"

"I thought you were having a tea party," Cade said, his arms dropping to his side. "What happened to champagne and chocolate—"

"Enough." She turned to her best friend. "Cade, this party is for my sister. Unless Lucia decides to share her favor with you, it's none of your business."

"Fair enough," Cade said, still frowning.

"Don't try to weasel clues out of the best man," she ordered. And then she turned to face Jack. "And you. Not another word about this afternoon."

She pushed past Cade and headed for her sister. And she kept her head high. Dammit, she'd won this round—even if it had left her wanting a late night visit from a SEAL.

Three flirtatious waiters. Two tipsy social workers. And one drunken mother of the groom. Natalie scanned the private party room at Chocolatini. The bachelorette party site wasn't that much different than Bottom's Up—apart from the drunken mother of the groom and the scenery. The floor to ceiling windows looking out over the Strip offered a better view than her bar in Coronado. And the velvet couches and low coffee tables would have looked ridiculous alongside her wooden barstools.

But if she kept telling herself it was the same, maybe she wouldn't feel so out of place attending the party instead of serving the drinks.

A shirtless man—another sight she generally only witnessed at Bottom's Up during a bar fight between hotheaded, drunken sailors—flashed a smile as he delivered yet another pitcher of "tea" to her sister's giggling coworkers. Lucia had moved to California a little over a year ago, and while she'd made a few friends, there were only a handful she'd felt comfortable inviting to a destination wedding. Her sister claimed she wanted to keep it small—one maid of honor, no bridesmaids for the wedding party. But Natalie had a hunch her sister didn't exactly have a lot of friends from her years spent in Tennessee.

"When I made the reservation," Natalie said, leaning closer to her sister, "I didn't realize they served rum punch in the teapots."

"I don't think Cade's mother did either," Lucia said, frowning at the slim, silver-haired woman, who was about three minutes away from falling asleep on one of the sofas. "Or maybe it's the jet lag."

The waiter stopped in front of their sofa. "Another special daiquiri for our bride-to-be. With two umbrellas. And a beer for the maid of honor."

"Thank you." Lucia accepted the drinks. Her sister thrust

the beer into her hand as the waiter slipped out of earshot.

"Do you think his muscles are better than Jack's?" her sister asked.

"Well, Jack doesn't rub baby oil all over himself, so I'd say Jack wins this one," Natalie said. "But maybe if you gave the waiter a bath… No, he'd still look like a gym rat compared to the type of guy who hunts down bad guys."

"So you've seen Jack's muscles up close and personal," Lucia said.

"So have you." Natalie raised her beer to her lips and took a sip while her sister's eyes widened. "At the pool yesterday, all of the SEALs were walking around without their shirts at some point."

"I had the impression you saw more," her sister said. "Yesterday in his room?"

So much more.

And while she'd never forget the way he looked on his knees in the entryway, or the way his hands felt on her breasts in the shower…she couldn't risk another private look at Jack's muscles. Not if she wanted to win the bet.

Remember the sweet taste of victory.

"He helped me with some shopping." Natalie stood and pulled out the plastic bag she'd tucked behind the sofa. "I have party favors. There are extras if you want two."

Lucia plucked a wrapped can from the bag and tore into the tissue paper. She tossed the wrapping aside, and then her eyes quickly filled with unshed tears. "Chocolate body paint," she murmured, her voice trembling.

Most brides went a little crazy before the wedding. But tears over what was essentially a gag gift at the bachelorette party?

"Were you really hoping for plastic penis straws? Or did you have a bad experience with body paint once?" Natalie asked as she reclaimed her spot on the sofa beside her sister.

Thank God they hadn't unwrapped the favors in front of Lucia's tipsy coworkers.

"No, I've never used body paint." Her sister bit her lower lip. "Well, not real body paint—"

"Stop right there," Natalie warned. There were some things she never, ever needed to hear.

Lucia laughed, wiping away the tears. "Before I met Cade, I never thought I'd have a reason to use this kind of paint. Finding someone who saw beyond the scars—it felt impossible."

"I'm so sorry that you had to live like that for so long," Natalie said, the familiar guilt rising up and taking hold of her. She didn't wear the same physical scars, but "impossible" maintained a tangible presence in her life. The thought of letting someone in—it felt unattainable.

"It's not your fault." Lucia lifted the "special" daiquiri to her lips and drained the drink.

"Yes, it is," Natalie said, her voice firm. "If I hadn't left that day. Or if I'd tried harder with the other families…"

Lucia reached out and took her hand. "Stop. Please. I hid behind my fears. I decided to live a lonely life. But then I met Cade and…" A dreamy smile spread across her face.

Natalie narrowed her gaze and focused on the empty daiquiri glass. How many fruity cocktails had Lucia ordered from the baby-oiled waiters?

"I just hope that you'll find someone who helps you lock the past where it belongs," her sister continued. "Someone who makes you happy and helps you to look to the future."

"I'm not like you," Natalie said. "I'm the reason the first two families gave up on us. If I'd simply bowed to their authority instead of trying to fight them every step of the way. If I'd tried—"

"Maybe I would have been spared a few lonely years. Maybe not." Lucia shrugged. "But maybe I wouldn't have met

Cade. And I can't imagine my world without him."

"I'm glad it all worked out," Natalie said, pulling her hand free and reaching for her beer. There had been so many moments when it could have gone oh so wrong.

The wistful look returned, accompanied by a giggle. "You have no idea," Lucia said.

"Are you drunk?" Natalie asked. It was her sister's party. She had every right to pass out under the table if she wanted. But they should probably save the heart-to-hearts for when her sister was sober. "I know you've avoided the 'tea,' but what's in those special daiquiris?"

Lucia leaned closer and whispered, "Promise you won't tell?"

Natalie nodded.

"They're virgin daiquiris," she quietly said. "I'm pregnant."

"You're having a baby? Oh my God, Lucia!" She reached for her sister and wrapped her arms around her. And she buried her face against Lucia's shoulder as she tumbled off an emotional cliff.

"You can't tell anyone. It's still early," Lucia said. "And we honestly weren't expecting it to happen this fast. I mean, Cade was home for a few days six weeks ago and we talked about it, decided we didn't want to wait much longer. That night, we skipped protection. And it worked."

"I won't say a word," she promised. "And I'm so happy for you. If this is what you want—"

"It is," her sister said firmly. "I want to start a family with Cade. It won't be easy. He'll be gone a lot. But I know the good moments will make it all worth it."

The good moments. Her sister said those words and Natalie pictured Jack in the shower, touching her, teasing her…

But it was only a taste of happiness.

"You should have it all," Natalie said firmly. "And I'll be

there to help you. I'll be the best aunt." She closed her eyes, fighting back tears. She meant it, every word.

"I know you will. Natalie, it feels like a dream. A really good one. Even better than Cade covered in chocolate body paint."

Natalie pulled back. "That's something I don't want to think about. The father of my future niece or nephew." She forced a laugh, but it sounded brittle. Her sister was bubbling with happiness, but that joy…

For her, it still felt out of reach.

"You could be dreaming about painting your very own SEAL in chocolate," Lucia said, holding up the container.

Every time I close my eyes.

But that wicked fantasy didn't lead to wedding bells and babies. Not for her.

"If you'd just give Jack a shot," her sister continued. "I think he really likes you. You've been spending a lot of time with him since you arrived."

Because there's this bet I haven't told you about…

But now, on the heels of her sister's happy announcement, wasn't the time to tell her about the bet. Still, the thought of losing herself in his touch, his kiss, in *him*. It was tempting to run away from the emotions inspired by her sister's announcement and straight into Jack's arms.

But how many times could she abandon her clothes, steal a taste of all the charming SEAL had to offer, and walk away the winner?

"No." Natalie shook her head. "I'm better off on my own."

Unless I want to forget my resolve and let him win…

She pictured Jack standing naked and very aroused in the entryway to his suite. Losing might feel very, *very* good…

"Chocolate body paint?" One of the tipsy social workers cried as she pushed off the couch and stumbled toward them. "Do you think Rick will let us try it on his abs?"

"The waiter," the other drunken coworker explained as she turned to Lucia. "You can't tell anyone at the hospital about this. But OMG, I want to lick chocolate off that man's body."

Lucia laughed and smiled at her friends. "My lips are sealed."

Natalie smiled and tried to bottle up her ugly feelings. Lucia had suffered through so much. Her sister deserved to find happiness with her growing family. But next to Lucia's I'm-in-love-and-pregnant glow, Natalie felt like she'd been thrust deeper into the deep, dark forest of loneliness.

She'd experienced a moment of genuine happiness with Jack. But the thought of loving a man, letting him into her life, and then sending him off to fight, not knowing if he'd ever come back...

She'd fall apart if she opened her heart to him and then lost him. That was the only given in this equation. Maybe other wives and girlfriends saw the glass as half full. These were highly trained soldiers. They were good at what they did. The best. There was a good chance they were coming home.

But she'd stopped seeing the glass as half full a long time ago. People died every day in car crashes, leaving their kids behind. One stupid teenage rebellion, one trip to town, and a monster of a man had attacked her sister.

She couldn't do it. She couldn't have a relationship with Jack, especially not a long-term one. Maybe her sister believed she could face anything, including Cade's long deployments, after what they'd been through. But Natalie refused to set herself up for heartache.

And that was if Jack wanted anything more than to win a bet. Which was a pretty damn big "if."

Natalie leaned in to her sister. "I might not have all the answers, but I know that I have no desire to find out what baby oil mixed with chocolate body paint tastes like. If you don't need me here, I'm going to check on Mufasa."

"Go." Lucia waved her off. "I'll take care of them. And if you happen to bump into a certain SEAL…"

Natalie forced a smile. "Thanks, but that's not going to happen."

Prince Charming wasn't roaming the hotel halls, waiting for her. Even if he was, he wasn't her ticket to happy ever after.

But he could be your ticket to another orgasm. He could take the edge off the loneliness.

She reached the exit and glanced back at Lucia, her beautiful, glowing, pregnant sister. She should return to the party. She should smile, laugh, and pretend the lonesomeness wasn't threatening to swallow her whole.

But it was.

She turned and pushed through the door. Heaven help her if she ran into Jack now. She might give in and let him win. Right now, she'd risk losing for another taste of the happiness she'd felt in his shower. It would kill her to truly give in to him, to let him claim her in the way she knew he wanted, but she was close to drowning in the surge of memory and pain. If the only way to keep her head above water was to get lost in him, she wouldn't resist.

Chapter Fourteen

All Jack needed was a fucking crown. Then he would be the official King of Stupid. Only the kingdom's ruler would bet his brothers that he could talk the woman of his fantasies into his bed—in front of her—and then continue to play truth or dare with her.

Except they'd never touched on truth, they were playing dare or dare. After that first night—when she'd hightailed it out of dinner, and then come screaming his name through the bathroom door, offering one helluva clue that she wanted him, too—after that, he should have changed the rules of the game to truth or truth in an attempt to start something real.

And miss out on the best blow job in the history of blow jobs.

Jack stopped in the middle of the empty hallway. Yeah, that sounded pretty damn stupid, too.

But he knew they had to talk. He needed to admit the truth. This wasn't just a bet. He wanted more than one night with her. And he needed to find out why she'd refused to give him a shot when it was kind of obvious she wanted him too.

He headed down the long winding hall toward Natalie's room in the most undesirable corner of the hotel. Only a person smuggling a giant dog in and out three or four times a day would request a room by the stairwell and the catering supply storage. To be fair, she probably didn't know about the catering supply area when she'd checked in.

He rounded the corner and reached the second set of elevator banks. One set of shiny gold doors opened and out stepped Natalie. She'd traded her bartender's uniform—jeans, fitted shirt, the occasional skirt that threatened to blow his mind—for a black sundress with thin straps. The top hugged her chest, while the skirt flowed around her legs, stopping above the knee. By Vegas standards, she looked ready for church. But one look and Jack knew precisely where he wanted to see her dress—the bedroom floor.

"Jack?" She froze just out of arm's reach. "Are you lost? Trust me, the rooms on this floor are nothing like yours."

"I came—" *To help with your dog. Because Cade sent me. Oh, and the wedding toasts, we should work on those.* "I wanted to talk to you," he said.

"If that's your new strategy…" She shook her head and drew a deep breath. "Please, I can't do this right now."

Her shoulders hunched forward as she studied the floor. Where was the feisty bartender who could take on a room of drunken sailors? The woman who never begged? The woman who declared victory after a shower?

"Natalie?" He stepped in front of her and was a hair's breadth away from pulling her into his arms when she shoved her hands into pockets hidden in the folds of her dress.

"I need to check on my dog," she said, trying to move past him.

But he couldn't let her run away. Not like this. He stepped in front of her, careful to still give her space. He wouldn't reach for her or touch her.

"What happened?" he asked. She looked up, and he saw the tears threatening in her eyes. "Please tell me."

"Sometimes I look at my sister and I see all the mistakes I've made." She spoke softly, her brown eyes staring into his. "She's so happy now. Against all the odds, after everything that happened to us, to her…she's moved on."

She bit her lip and dipped her chin to her chest, lowering her gaze to the floor.

"Natalie." He closed the space between them and placed his hands on her arms. "Look at me."

She tensed beneath his grip. But this time, she listened. Her brown eyes glanced at him from under her long lashes. And he knew he had about five seconds before she made the call—fight or flight. Right now, neither worked in his favor.

"There's no reason you can't be happy, too," he said, keeping his tone soft and gentle, as if she were a stray kitten that simply needed a little love and a good home.

She placed her hands on his chest and damn near shocked the hell out of him. Flight—ten to one he'd thought she'd race for her room. But instead she ran her hands over his shoulder and up to his jaw.

"Is that your new tactic?" She touched the sides of his face as if she enjoyed the feel of his stubble scratching her palms. "Planning to win by promising me—"

"No," he said firmly.

"Because it might work." She inhaled and appeared surprised she'd let those words escape. But then, she stepped closer, pressing her body flush against his. "Right now, I want to get lost in you."

"Natalie." The way he said her name—shit, having the woman of his dreams touch him hadn't damaged his hearing. He knew that when he said her name it sounded a helluva lot like *I want you*, not *Let's talk*.

"I feel safe with you, Jack," she said. "Not because you're

a SEAL. But because you're *you*."

He sighed. And shit, he tried to mask his *Oh darlin' that's the sweetest thing anyone has ever said to me* reaction by reaching for her. He wrapped his hands around her hips and pulled her against him.

He knew she felt safe with him because she knew he was temporary. That whatever happened between them now, it would go no further. He'd never before been so happy yet so crushed to know who he was and what he could—and couldn't—offer a woman.

"You are safe," he promised.

Her gaze dropped to his lips. "I'd planned to find someone else," she said. "In Vegas. For sex. To fight this…this *thing* between us. To fight everything."

What the fuck?

"That's not going to happen." He rocked his hips into her, letting her feel how damn hard he was for her. He was seconds away from abandoning his plans to freaking talk to her and instead push her up against a wall. He wanted to take her right here, by the damn elevator bank. But he knew security cameras monitored this hallway. And the thought of anyone else seeing her face as she came for *him*? Not a chance. He'd get them to her damn room.

"I haven't had sex in a long time," she said. "And I thought that if I did, with someone else…"

He growled and took a step backward. He maintained a strong hold on her as he steered them away from the elevators and down the hall.

"But for some stupid reason, I don't want someone else," she said, allowing him to lead their dance down the empty hall. "I want your cock—"

Yeah, talking would have to wait until he gave Natalie every damn thing her heart desired.

"Your baby-oil-free muscles—"

"What?" He stopped ten feet from her bedroom door. Was Vegas messing with her fantasies?

"Your mouth." She rose up on her tiptoes and pressed her lips to his. Not a gentle brush of the lips, but a demanding, let's-get-naked kiss. Her fingers moved through his hair, holding his head tight. And he kissed her right back, determined to erase any lingering thoughts of her imaginary, baby-oil-covered lover.

His tongue tangled with hers, teasing, taunting, and asking for more. She pressed up against him, forcing him back, one step after another, until—shit, they bumped into a wall.

But the woman on fire in his arms, her lips still moving over his, didn't care. She straddled his thigh and began to rock her hips. His hands traveled down from her hips to the smooth, bare skin of her thighs. And that was all the confirmation he needed. Her dress was too damn close to decorating her waist. As much as he wanted to hear her come, they weren't doing this here.

In the hall.

On camera.

"Your room key," he demanded, breaking the kiss. He tried to smooth her skirt down over her legs, but she'd spread them too far. And she refused to stop riding his leg.

"In my pocket," she said, breathing heavy.

Looking down at the bunched-up black fabric and the smooth bodice, he ran his hands over her waist, searching and searching...bingo! He found an opening in her dress and slipped his hand inside, retrieving the key card.

He shifted away from the wall and reached his hands under her perfect ass. His hands touched her cotton panties, tempting him to explore. But his number one priority was getting Natalie into her room. He lifted her up and fought back a curse as she wrapped her legs around him. And then he took off for her room at the very end of the damn hall.

He reached the door, opened it, and carried her inside, silently thanking the Navy for all those hours of physical training. He leaned back against the door and lowered her down to the floor.

Woof!

Shit, they'd escaped the too public hallway before losing their clothes, but now they had a hundred-something-pound dog to manage. He looked down at Natalie. Those full lips— he wanted to kiss her as he stripped off her dress. He wanted to sink into her and give her the one thing she wanted from him. His cock. Because wasn't that a miracle? After years of fantasizing about her, watching and wishing he could make her *his*, she'd walked up to him and offered to make his dreams come true.

Woof!

But first—

"Do we need to take the dog out?" he asked.

"He'll settle down," she said, slipping her hands beneath his T-shirt and running her palms over his abs. "I took him out earlier."

His jaw clenched as she brushed his nipples. He'd never been happier to hear those words.

"And this won't take long," she added, stepping her feet apart until the wet fabric of her panties pressed against his thigh. He could feel just how damn ready she was through his cargo shorts.

"Is that a challenge?" he asked. He wanted to draw this out, make this moment last.

"No. I'm just so close." She rocked her hips, riding him in earnest. "Hold on to me. Please, Jack."

He ran his hands up her thighs, lifting her dress to her waist. He felt like a teenager, driving her closer and closer to an orgasm with layers of clothes still between them. But even though she'd issued a warning—*orgasm approaching!*—he planned to draw this out.

He ran his hands over her ass, first on the outside of her underwear and then beneath. His dick pressed against his fly, begging to join the party. But first he wanted to touch her. He gave her ass a light squeeze.

"Oh God!" she cried, her fingers digging into his chest. Her hips rocked back and forth, searching for release.

Shit, I'll have to add that to the mental list of ways she likes to be touched.

"Look at me," he said, his gaze locking with hers. "Every time I walk into your bar, I'm going to picture you like this. Writhing, ready, so desperate to come. Darlin', I'll wait until your shift ends. Then I'll take you into the back room."

"This time," she gasped, "I'm going to tie you up."

"Is that how you like it?" His grip tightened on her ass. But her hips bucked, fighting his control. Still, he held tight and pulled her against his thigh. "I don't know, Natalie, I think you like the idea of me calling the shots."

"No, I...oh Jack!" she cried. "I can't...it's too...oh, wow!"

His lips parted as he leaned against the door, bracing his body to take the full force of the wild, wanton, screaming woman coming hard against his thigh.

"That..." she murmured as her movements slowed. Her hips maintained a gentle thrust against him, as if she wanted to ride out the aftershocks. "That was so close to perfect."

And shit, he wished that were true. But there was so much left unspoken. So much left undone.

"I think we can do better," he said, issuing a challenge because he needed to keep her here, with him.

"I don't know. I'm going to remember that orgasm for a long time," she said, stepping away and leaving behind a very wet spot on his leg. Her brown eyes shone wild and bright as she smiled at him. "And I bet you will, too. What just happened—it would make a great bedtime story. If you're alone and need…"

He raised an eyebrow as he pressed his hand against the front of his cargo shorts.

She laughed as she reached behind her. One second the black dress was holding tight to her breasts, and the next, it was decorating the floor at her feet.

"What do you say, Prince Charming? Ready to create another naughty story?"

Chapter Fifteen

"**P**rince Charming?"

Jack directed the words at her breasts. And she couldn't blame him. She'd walked off the elevator and thrown herself at him, desperate to feel anything other than the lingering hurts from her past. She'd focused on the need building in her body, demanding an orgasm.

She'd told him she wanted his cock and then proceeded to use him as her personal sex toy. Maybe that made her a horrible person. But how much lower could she go on the awful-person scale? As a teen, she'd driven away every foster family who tried to care for her and Lucia. She'd pushed her sister away after the incident because she couldn't find a way to solve Lucia's hurt. And she'd guarded her heart to the point that she'd locked it up and buried the key.

"Natalie," he said.

She focused on his voice, his words, and the way he moved his hand over the front of his shorts. She pushed the questions away, saving them for a time when she didn't have an orgasm-inducing Navy SEAL in her bedroom. The loneliness couldn't touch her. Not when he was here, looking like he wanted to devour her.

"What about the bedtime version of little red riding hood and the big bad wolf?" She slipped off her underwear. "We could take turns playing the wolf. Or you could be the hero who rushes in to save the day."

"I'm not your Prince Charming. You made it clear yesterday that I'm just a man." He grabbed the fabric at the back of his neck and drew his shirt over his head.

"It's my nickname for you," she admitted. "You're good with words."

He froze with his thumbs hooked into the top of his jeans. "About that. I honestly came here to talk."

She focused on his hands, not wanting to look at his face. He was here to win a bet. If he told her otherwise, she would have to kick the half-naked, very hard Navy SEAL out of her bedroom. If he wanted more than a win, if he wanted her to unlock her heart—

No, this only worked if the silent promise stood between them. This was a game. He wasn't here to claim her and keep her in his life. She couldn't open herself up to that possibility.

"Forget the fairy tales," she said.

He shook his head. "That's not what I meant."

"Take off your pants and climb on the bed," she ordered. "Listen to me. And you just might win."

She'd accept defeat on this one. Bringing him to his knees and walking away—that plan had one major flaw. She wanted to run toward him, dragging him to her bed. Maybe she couldn't have the happy-ever-after ending. But she could have these moments locked away in her memory.

"I didn't come here because of that stupid bet," he said, placing his hands on his hips.

"You don't want to win?" she challenged, shifting her weight. She refused to run away. This was her room. But he needed to lose the clothes. Standing completely naked in front of a half-dressed man left her too close to vulnerable. "To beat your brothers?"

"I do," he said. The muscles in his arms flexed as if he was working overtime to keep from reaching for her. "But I want you—"

"Then come get me," she demanded. She didn't need to hear any more. He wanted her, and she might lose her mind if she didn't feel this man inside her soon. Now. She needed him *now*. Before she changed her mind. Before she woke up to the fact that sex with him might leave her stranded on the road labeled hurt. And if she lost her footing, she might stumble head over heels into rejection.

She turned and climbed on the bed. She stretched her arms overhead and reached for the headboard, then arched her back, thrusting her breasts up into the air.

"Ah, hell," he said.

She heard a rustling. Keeping her arms overhead, she lifted her head and watched as the naked SEAL set his sights on her. He held a condom in one hand.

"Good to know we're on the same page," she said as he reached the foot of the bed.

"Are we?" He tossed the condom beside her on the bed and raised an eyebrow.

"Need help putting it on?" She nodded her head to the square packet resting by her left hip.

"We'll get there." His gaze ran up and down her body.

Was he debating where to start? Not that it was his call…

"I'm ready for you *now*," she said. "I don't need more foreplay."

"What about me?" He wrapped his hand around the base of his cock. "I need a warm-up."

She stared at his long, thick cock standing at attention as she drew her knees up and planted her feet on the bed.

"You only need to answer one question, Jack. Do you like me like this?" She rocked her hips up as her feet pressed into the bedding. "Or like this?" She lowered her hips and straightened her legs until her feet reached opposite corners of the bed.

"Like that," he growled.

Maybe she looked ready and willing to submit with her legs spread as if bound by imaginary satin sashes to opposite corners of the bed, and her arms reaching overhead. But nothing was holding her down. And she was still calling the shots.

"I dare you to climb up on the bed," she said. "And let me prove you wrong. We're done playing."

"We are?" He placed one knee on the bed between her spread legs. Then he reached up and placed one hand on either side of her breasts. His other knee touched the bed as he shifted his upper body over her. Slowly, he lowered his hips until his cock brushed the trimmed curls between her legs.

"You need a condom," she said, forcing her eyes to remain open, her gaze locked with his. She wouldn't be the first one to look away and lose herself in the moment.

"Not just yet."

"Jack—"

He allowed his hard length to slide back and forth over her, teasing her clit. And she gasped.

"Don't move, Natalie. Let me play."

She tilted her hips and felt his cock glide over the part of her body that was wet and ready to draw him in. Smiling down at her, he pinned her to the bed with his lower body.

"I wish I had those black silk ties right now," he murmured, shifting back and forth without offering her room to move.

She gritted her teeth, fighting back the threatening orgasm. But oh God, with his cock swirling over her clit…the mental picture from his story…those ties…

"Condom," she gasped, lowering her hand and searching the bedspread beside her hip for the packet. "Now."

"Not yet," he growled.

He rocked faster and faster, pushing her so close to coming. But she couldn't let him win this round. Abandoning her search for the condom, she waited until he lifted his hips and reached between them. She wrapped her fingers around his wet, slick cock and began to pump, gliding her thumb through the moisture at the top.

"You're ready." She kept her eyes locked on his face, watching as his resolution faded. "You don't need a warm-up."

"Fuck." He closed his eyes and let his head fall back. His biceps bulged as he worked to keep his upper body off her and thrust his hips into her hand. Once. Twice. And then he groaned as he came.

I win this round. The warm-up round.

She eased her hand out from between their bodies.

But once you recover, I'm going to let you win the game and claim victory.

Chapter Sixteen

*F**uck me.*

And yeah, that was pretty much his only coherent thought as pleasure ripped through him. Once he was spent, he collapsed on the bed by her side.

Shit, maybe she did have the ultimate control, because instead of talking or sinking into her and making her come a second time, he'd exploded in her freaking hand.

"Ten minutes," he murmured. "And then it is game on again." He had to redeem himself after that little performance. "This time, we do it my way."

"Hmm, well, your way didn't get the job done," she said.

"Is that another challenge?" he asked, turning on his side to look at her. He pressed his elbow into the mattress and allowed his head to rest against his hand. She'd dropped her hands to her sides, but he kept her legs straight and spread in a narrow V.

"Observation," she murmured.

She turned her head toward him. The heat in her eyes sent a loud and clear message to his still recovering body—

You got yours, but I'm still primed and ready for my second big O.

What if he pushed to do this his way? What if he demanded control? Would she run for the bathroom door?

With the questions rushing rapid-fire through his mind, he watched as she slid her hand over her breasts and traced a path down her taut stomach to her dark, wet curls. Her index finger slipped between her folds, and her back arched.

No, this woman wouldn't run and hide. But she just might kick him out. And he wasn't looking for a repeat of the motel room in the middle of nowhere California. He refused to settle for listening to her moan and cry out through another goddamn door, not when she'd already let him inside.

Speaking of…

Why did she let me in?

Her eyes fluttered closed as she drew her knees up, opening her body and granting her fingers access.

To torture me, he thought, willing his dick to recover and get back in the game.

"Natalie, don't even think about crossing the finish line without me," he said. "I like watching you. Hell, I love it. But I don't want to walk out of here until I've felt you fall apart while I'm buried deep inside you."

She opened her eyes, granting him at least a part of her attention. Her fingers continued to move between her legs. And for a second, he swore he saw a hint of vulnerability—as though she'd opened herself up to more than his touch.

"I won't," she said. And instead of fighting him, pushing back and demanding to give the orders, she withdrew her wet fingers.

He froze and waited to see what she'd do next. But she simply let her hand fall to her side, leaving her body open and waiting for him. And his dick begged to accept the invitation.

He studied her face as he reached for a condom. Her

big brown eyes, her full lips—he knew her. Shit, her face had haunted his dreams for so damn long. But right now, she didn't look like the don't-you-dare-give-me-any-shit woman who managed a bar full of sailors and soldiers. "Are you sure?" he asked.

"I won't—"

"I'm not asking you to beg," he said quickly. "But if you're having second thoughts, please tell me."

She pressed her lips together into a thin line. And Jack held his breath.

Please tell me you want this. I'll walk away if you ask me to go. From the fantasy, from you. But—

"Are *you* having second thoughts?" she challenged, the fire returning to her brown eyes.

"No." He tore open the condom and rolled it onto his very grateful dick. "How can I make you come? What will make you scream my name? That's all I'm thinking about right now."

Later, he'd worry about why she'd let him in, granting him a peek beneath her tough-girl exterior.

"Good," she said, reaching her arms overhead.

And hell if that wasn't an invitation to cover her body with his. He knelt between her splayed legs. Placing one hand on the mattress beside her, he used the other to position himself at her entrance. And then he pushed inside.

"Fuck," he gasped, holding himself still and giving her time to adjust. She was so damn tight.

"Don't stop," she said, rocking her hips beneath him. "I haven't done this in a while, so make it good. Okay?"

"Planning to." He held back the question: *How long?* Because he knew she was close to begging. If he pushed her over that line, she'd never forgive him. And if he did anything to prematurely end this, he'd kick his own damn ass. He'd never been so grateful for a pre-game hand job.

Gentle.

The word flashed in his mind like a freaking neon sign. Leaning on one elbow, he ran his free hand over her jaw and down her throat. He kept his touch light, moving south to her breasts.

"Jack?" She moaned his name as she gripped his shoulders. Her fingers dug into his skin.

Fuck—someone missed the flashing gentle sign.

"Yeah?" he gasped. It was a miracle he managed that one word with her nails running over his back and down to his ass. Her touch rode the line between sweet, sweet pleasure and the bite of pain. He was about five seconds away from ignoring the neon warning.

"I'm not breakable," she whispered.

He stared down into her brown eyes. She raised an eyebrow—an unspoken challenge. And hell, she knew he couldn't turn away once she'd thrown down the gauntlet.

Abandoning her breasts, he reached down and guided her leg up until it wrapped around him. "Hold on tight, darlin'."

And then he began to move. He thrust in and out, holding nothing back. Fucking missionary had never felt so good.

Next time, I'll get creative. Doggie style. Reverse cowgirl. Next time—

"More!" She arched her back and lifted her hips up to meet him thrust for thrust. Her nails clawed at his back as if determined to leave marks. "More, for the love of…oh God, Jack!"

He went for it, pushing into her harder, faster, giving more until he'd left gentle so far behind he wasn't sure he remembered the meaning of the word. And then—*fuck.* He closed his eyes against the explosion ripping through him.

"Jack!"

She was right there with him, her body convulsing around him as he came. As his orgasm ebbed, she placed her hands on his chest and pushed. He rolled onto his back and she went with him, her legs straddling his hips, their bodies still joined. He looked up at the beautiful woman riding him for damn near all he was worth.

Her long hair fell over her shoulders, teasing her perfect, perky tits. Her lips parted as she gasped and moaned.

Breathtaking. Fucking breathtaking.

He didn't have much left to give, but damn if she didn't take and take…

"Oh, wow," she groaned as her head fell back and her body fell apart. She trembled around him. Then she released her grip on his pecs and collapsed on his chest, completely spent.

"You won," she said, her head resting against his shoulder.

I won?

"The bet," she added, her breathing still uneven as he ran his hands up and down her upper arms.

"Yeah," he murmured. But why did victory suddenly feel like a swift punch to the gut?

"I should get up." She pressed her hands against his chest like she was preparing to launch off of him.

"Stay." He wrapped his arms around her, tightening his hold. "Please."

"I should check on my dog."

She pulled away from him, and this time he let her go, his arms falling to his sides. He sat up and watched as she gathered her clothes and headed for the hundred-plus-pound dog in the bathroom.

He'd won. But for the first time since he'd turned five, beating his brothers didn't feel like a victory. Because the woman who up until today had fought this thing between them—this let's get naked now pull—she'd left him wishing for another peek beneath the tough-girl exterior she wore like a shield.

Natalie looked back at him and offered a smile. "We can toast your victory at the rehearsal dinner tonight. With the other SEALs."

"No," he said. But he was talking to an empty room. She'd already joined her dog on the other side of the door.

"Because you're the prize, Natalie," he added, knowing that he needed to find a way to say those words to her. "I was too caught up in the past and my stupid need to win that I couldn't see it. But it's always been you."

Chapter Seventeen

"It's over." Natalie pressed her back against the bathroom door. One more step inside the bathroom and she'd literally be standing on the dog sprawled across the floor. "It's done. He won. Now I can…"

Take her two orgasms—three if she counted riding his thigh until the friction caused her to combust—and what? Hope they returned to the status quo? She would serve him beers and listen to his stupid one-liners pretending she didn't want him to make her scream his name again?

She closed her eyes. She couldn't want that. Him. She didn't need—

Silk ties… Jack hovering over her… Taking her…

"It was just a bet," she whispered. She was not adding Jack to the list of people who'd walked away from her. Which was why *she* had walked away this time. She didn't need him in her life. She managed just fine without a charming SEAL trying to call the shots—and give her orgasms. Just fine.

Woof!

Natalie opened her eyes and focused on her dog. "I'd

break you out of here, but there's a naked SEAL on my bed."

And I can't leave this bathroom until I'm certain I won't burst into tears.

She bit her lip and searched through the ball of clothing she'd carried into the bathroom, looking for her phone. If she couldn't even say those words to her dog, chances were she'd fall apart in the hallway. Maybe she couldn't control her desire to tumble into bed with Jack, but she could make sure security didn't find her weeping beside the dog she'd snuck into their hotel.

She found her phone and dialed Cade.

"Natalie?" he answered after the first ring.

"I hate to interrupt. I know you're having drinks with the guys." *Minus Jack.* "But are you sober enough to smuggle your dog out of the hotel?"

"Yes," Cade said. She heard footsteps, but otherwise the background sounded oddly quiet for a bar. "Most of the guys bailed on drinks. I'm heading to my room now. I'll head your way instead. Be there in a minute."

"Better make it five," she said with a sigh. "Jack's here. And I should give him a few minutes to find his clothes."

The footsteps stopped. She waited for Cade to ask if she'd lost.

"Natalie?" he said. "Are you all right?"

"Fine," she said firmly.

"You're lying," her best friend said. "But we don't have to talk about it. If there's anyone I trust to take care of herself, it's you."

But I don't trust myself. Not around Jack.

She ended the call and set her phone by the bathroom sink.

Come on, Natalie. You can do this. Just steer clear of him until after the wedding.

And then this would all fade away. The memory of those

orgasms, the feel of his arms wrapped around her, the sound of his voice murmuring naughty things through the bathroom door—

"Natalie? Are you all right?" the man she planned to wipe from her memory called through the door.

"Yes," she said. Mufasa pushed himself off the ground, offering her a wide-eyed doggie version of the "oh really?" look.

"I'd like to talk to you," he said. And oh God, he was right there on the other side of the door.

"I'll see you at dinner tonight," she said. By then she'd be ready to face him, laugh with his teammates about his victory, and focus on surviving her sister's wedding day while wearing the world's ugliest bridesmaid dress.

A tear ran down her cheek, chased by another, and then another.

The Terrible Tutu.

Now that was something to cry about.

"What part of drinks in the bar with the groom during the bachelorette thing didn't you understand?" Ronan said, his tone downright serious. As the only officer in a group of enlisted SEALs, he sounded a helluva lot like he was pulling rank. And that damn near never happened unless they were on base or deployed.

"Cade's the reason we're here, spending our down time in the desert," Ronan added as he shifted his gaze from Dante and then back to Jack. The redheaded SEAL stood with his back to a floor to ceiling wine cooler lined with bottles turned on their sides.

"Give them a break," Cade said as he joined the group. As a rule, his teammate, and the man of the hour, wore one of three uniforms—battle dress uniform, his Navy whites, or cargo pants and a T-shirt. Sometimes Cade switched the last one up, replacing the pants with board shorts. But a suit? Cade's gray slacks and blazer screamed "special occasion," which sure as shit translated into "no fights." Not even friendly ones between teammates.

But Ronan ignored the suit-signal. "Where were you, Dante?"

"I had to watch a dancer fake an orgasm," Dante said, looking past Ronan to the red wine, not that he gave a shit about the overpriced bottles.

Cade's eyebrows shot up as if their recently divorced teammate had just revealed that he'd spent the afternoon painting his nails. And sure, maybe twelve months put the dramatic end of Dante's marriage square in the past. But—

"I know you're out of practice," Cade said, the first one to recover. "But if you're ready to get back in the game, you should keep your eye on the prize. Participating in the real deal."

"Fuck you," Dante said. "I met this girl and she invited me to her show."

"A private show?" Ronan asked, folding his arms in front of his chest.

"Not yet," Dante said. "But I bet I have a better chance of moving the show to my hotel room before Jack hits his deadline."

His teammates turned to him. And shit, Cade looked like he might grind his teeth down to nothing. Jack looked past them, scanning the private room in the back of the new, hip Italian restaurant. He didn't see Natalie. But he knew that if he had any hope of sitting down and talking to her, he needed to put an end to their current situation.

And yeah, he also wanted a repeat of this afternoon. Maybe a different position, or they could stick with straight up missionary. Though he wouldn't mind a detour through her Yoga Poses for Blow Jobs playbook.

"Jack?" Cade said.

"He knows he can't win this one," Dante said.

"You're right," Jack said. "I'm not going to win. Natalie, well shit, she's not into me."

Dante laughed. "You knew that before you took the bet. She's turned you down and tuned you out for years."

No, she's heard every word.

Jack shook his head. "I can't win. I saw her this afternoon and she made it clear... I know when to call it. And this bet is off. I lose."

"What happened?" Cade asked, his voice hard and challenging. "This afternoon—how did it go south?"

I fell for her.

"Nothing," Jack said, looking his friend straight in the eyes. There was a chance Natalie had already talked to Cade. But he trusted his teammate to keep his mouth shut and let the others think Natalie had kicked him out before they'd lost their clothes.

"Your brothers are going to give you hell," Ronan said mildly.

"Yeah," Jack agreed. "And I'm sorry about your fifty bucks."

Ronan shrugged. "I thought she liked you."

"What is this? Grade school? The cold shoulder is really a 'come chase me around the playground' signal?" Dante said with a laugh.

Yes. But the grown-up version of the "playground" involved a bed.

"This is Vegas, Jack," Dante continued, slapping him on the shoulder. "You'll find someone else to keep you company while we're on leave. That I'd bet money on."

He could have sworn Cade let out a growl. But Jack kept

his attention on Dante. "And what? Watch some chick fake it on stage?" Jack asked. "How the hell does that work? Was she naked?"

Dante's smile faded. "She's in this show. It's part modern dance, part acrobats. No stripping, I swear. Summer—she's not that kind of girl. She's a physical therapist who danced in college. She tried out for the show hoping to find a way to pay off her school bills. I met her at the pool this morning. She offered me a ticket, and I went thinking it would be fun to see her move on stage. This woman. Her body. Man, I had to see her in action."

"And then you found out modern dance meant fake orgasms?" Ronan asked.

"That's what it looked like to me," Dante said. "Between the sounds—"

Jack tuned his teammate out. He didn't need to hear the details of a dancer's erotic show. He'd witnessed the real thing earlier. They might have avoided the reasons for ending up in bed together, pretending it was all about the bet. But the end result was 100 percent authentic—times three.

Prince Charming had forfeited.

Natalie pressed her hand against the wine cellar's glass wall. She'd been a step away from turning the corner and entering the private dining area on the other side of the bottles when she'd heard Jack's voice.

I can't win this one. I saw her this afternoon and she made it clear... I know when to call it. And this bet is off. I lose.

She stared at the stack of pinot noir. Chief Jack Barnes, the Navy SEAL who never backed down from a challenge, who ran toward his attackers, not away, had said the word *lose.*

And it was a big fat lie.

He'd won.

She closed her eyes and her mind drifted back to her hotel room. Jack's body hovering over hers…his thick, hard cock sliding inside her…his hips moving faster and faster… and the way he'd held her afterward. He'd wrapped his arms around her and asked her to stay.

She opened her eyes, and a waitress holding a tray lined with champagne flutes materialized in front of her.

"May I offer you—"

"Yes." Natalie plucked a glass off her tray and raised it to her lips. The waitress's eyes widened, but then she quickly disappeared around the corner to serve the rehearsal dinner guests.

Including Jack, the man who'd erased her excuse for following her desire straight into his arms. The bet had been her safety net. Without it…

Why had he lied?

She stared into her champagne flute. Did she want to know the answer?

Yes. I need to know. Even if the truth hurts, I have to find out why he threw the bet.

Maybe he'd had enough. One afternoon and he was ready to move on. Sure, he'd told his teammates—including Cade— he'd lost while they were in public. But Jack had probably called his brothers before the dinner and told them a very different story.

Maybe not. Maybe he wants me. Not the bet. Or the win. Just me.

And just like that, the hope she'd kept in hibernation for years peeked out and looked straight toward another night with her charming SEAL.

Not mine.

That hope was a double-edged sword. Because she didn't want hope. She knew where that led. She'd open her heart to him, but eventually, he'd leave her. And she couldn't—wouldn't—let herself be abandoned ever again.

She downed the rest of her champagne. He couldn't be hers. Not her lover or her boyfriend. She'd stopped relying on others so long ago. Sure, she had Cade. But their friendship worked because he never pushed for more than she could give. Cade understood that her trust had limits.

She lowered her empty glass. She'd had so much ripped away from her. Her parents. Her first two foster families—just as she was starting to let them in. And then Lucia. One bad decision on her part, an escape to hang out with the other teenagers in her new town, and Lucia ended up hurt. Then separated from Natalie as she was sent off to heal.

And Natalie had been left alone and struggling with guilt. *Never again.*

She couldn't return to that place where people could hurt her—leave her.

And Jack would leave. He had his career. She'd watched Cade deploy mission after mission, close to three hundred days spent God knew where last year.

Even if he stayed in Coronado, he'd walk away from her sooner or later. The things he wanted...the words he used to spell out his desires...

Black silk ties.

"Natalie?" Lucia peeked around the edge of the wine cellar divider. "Are you okay?"

Clutching her empty glass, she buried the dirty images in the back of her mind and smiled at her sister. "Fine. Just gathering my courage to face your friends knowing they spent the afternoon licking chocolate off the waiters."

"It wasn't that exciting," Lucia said as she stepped around the corner and took Natalie's free hand. "The manager came out and reminded us that no outside food was allowed. I think that was her nice way of saying the waiters are paid to flirt, but they draw the line at becoming human lollipops. I bet your afternoon was much more exciting."

"It was fine," she said.

Lucia raised a well-groomed eyebrow. Her sister's makeup was perfect, drawing attention from the scars on her cheek. But the marks were still there. Not even the best makeup artist in Sin City could erase the past. It would follow them around forever.

But unlike her sister, Natalie wasn't sure she could drag her baggage forward into a happily-ever-after future. Not that she planned to try. Because according to Jack, this afternoon never happened.

Chapter Eighteen

"You've been avoiding me." Jack moved to her side and she slowed her pace, allowing the rest of the bridal party to blaze a trail through the hotel lobby toward the bar.

"I thought you might ask for a personalized thank-you," she said, stealing a glance at Jack. She'd spent most of dinner picking apart her salmon and wondering how it would feel to tear off his crisp white button-down dress shirt.

His lips formed a smile that threatened to dissolve her underwear. "And you forgot your pen and paper?"

"Not that kind of thank-you," she murmured as the rest of the group bypassed the elevator banks and disappeared around the corner.

He stopped in front of the up and down buttons. "I'm still feeling pretty grateful myself for this afternoon."

She shook her head. "Not for that. A thank-you for throwing the bet."

His smile faded and his brow furrowed. "Cade told you?"

"I overheard your conversation," she said. She probably owed him an apology for eavesdropping. But after what he'd said, after the way he'd misled his teammates, guilt was low on her list of feelings. "Cade knows you're lying," she added.

"I know." Jack leaned over and pressed the up button.

"What about drinks in the bar?" she asked. "Or do you need to call your brothers first?"

"Trust me, talking to my family is not part of my plan for tonight." His gaze locked with hers. "And when I do, I'm sticking to my story. I lost."

The elevator dinged. He took her hand and drew her inside the mirrored and thankfully empty space.

"Why?" she demanded as the door closed. "You won. Why would you let Colton believe he beat you?"

"Because..." He stepped forward, guiding her back against the elevator wall. She pressed her palms against the mirrored surface as his gaze dropped to her mouth. He leaned in, and she closed her eyes, waiting for a kiss. But his lips bypassed hers and brushed up against her ear. "Because I've spent the last hour sitting across the table from you wishing that I could pull these straps down." He ran his hands up her bare arms to the spaghetti straps and dipped his index finger under the fabric.

"You didn't have to pretend you lost—" She gasped as he drew the straps down her shoulders. "For this."

"Yes, I did." His fingers teased the bare skin above her dress. "I like seeing you in a dress instead of your work jeans."

Was it really as simple as that? Did he just want her for sex after all? Part of her yearned for that simplicity, even as the other part yearned to know that he cared for her, even if just for a moment.

"After this weekend..." She gasped as his finger dipped beneath the neckline. "It's back to bar clothes." "I spent the entire main course wondering if you were wearing a bra. You weren't earlier." His hand moved lower, drawing the front of her dress down. If he kept that up, the top of her sundress would be decorating her waist—and offering the security cameras quite a show.

"I'm not." She gave him a little push as the elevator stopped and the doors opened.

"I know." Abandoning her breasts, he wrapped his arms around her waist and took her with him as he backed out of the elevator.

"What are you doing?" she whispered, looking up at his face.

"I barely heard a word of the speeches tonight," he said, turning their bodies, continuing to move backward down the hall—his hall, toward his room.

"Me neither," she admitted. "I was thinking about how you forfeited the bet."

"Yeah, the bet was close to the last thing on my mind." He kept her close, as if they were slow dancing through the hotel's mazelike interior to her room. "I wanted to send everyone out of the dining room and pull you onto my lap. I'd have lifted your dress to your waist, torn your underwear off you, and begged you to ride me. Cowgirl. Reverse cowgirl. I don't give a damn. I wanted you, Natalie."

Cowgirl—her on top, setting the rhythm and driving them both over the edge. She wanted the power to decide how fast and how deep he thrust into her. But would he hand over control?

"You'd never give up control," she said as they approached his bedroom door, clinging to remains of the crumbling barricade between them. Even without the bet, they wanted different things.

"I don't need to call the shots." He spoke those words with the determination of a man who went into battle focused on winning. He'd never planned to lose. Ever.

Until today.

"That's your training talking," she said as he drew to a

halt and released her to retrieve his key and open the door. "A SEAL never backs down."

He held open the door to his suite. "Try me."

And give him a chance to prove that they might work, not because of a bet, but because they wanted each other? No. She couldn't step inside. His sexual fantasy for tonight might offer her the illusion of control, allowing her to ride him. But he'd brought her here to stake a claim. Bet or no bet, he wanted her. And he wished to take her on his terms.

I want that, too.

But she was too afraid of the unknown. Where would he put his mouth next? And worse, would it lead to him stealing her heart?

She couldn't blindly follow him down that path, waiting until she stumbled into hurt at the end of the road. Yes, he wanted her today, but it was only a matter of time before he didn't want her—or worse, before he left on a mission and didn't return.

But what if she called the shots? One more night, following her rules, and in the morning, she walked away and returned to her controlled, and yes, lonely life. Before he decided she was too difficult. Too headstrong. Before any more gut-wrenching loss rained down on her.

"Jack." She ran her tongue over her lower lip. Could she do this? Demand a night with this man on her terms?

"I'm listening," he said, smiling at her, excitement bright and vibrant in his blue eyes.

"I dare you to let me tell the story tonight," she said, her voice firm.

His too charming grin widened. "Start talking, darlin'."

She summoned her courage, allowing her desire to simmer as she stepped into the room. She waited for him to close the door. Standing in the entryway where he'd fallen to his knees and licked her—just yesterday—she turned to face him. "Once upon a time, there was a girl—"

"Princess," he corrected, his fingers releasing the buttons on his shirt one by one.

"It's my story." She kicked off her sandals.

"And you should get to be a princess," he said, placing his hands on his hips. His shirt hung open, revealing the hard lines of his sculpted chest.

"Once upon a time, there was *a girl* who kept her fantasies locked away. Sometimes, while alone with her toys…" She let that image linger between them.

"You're killing me, darlin'." He stripped off his dress shirt and tossed it aside. "Tell me more."

"Sometimes she would close her eyes and let the fantasies play out in her mind." Natalie reached under her dress and hooked her thumbs in her panties. Slowly, she drew them down her legs. "This girl, she pictured a naked warrior, the kind of man with muscles that screamed *I never give up* lying on her bed. He kept his feet planted on the ground and his back against the mattress. This warrior, he was hard and ready to offer her exactly what she needed."

She paused and stepped out of her underwear, leaving it on the floor.

"What did she need?" Jack asked, keeping his gaze fixed on her abandoned panties.

"Take off your pants and go sit on the bed," she ordered. She held tight to her confidence. Would she win this round? Or would he say to hell with the dare and take control of her story?

His hand moved to the button on his dress slacks. Her eyes widened as he removed his shoes, socks, and pants. But on his way to the bed, he took a detour to his rucksack.

"Jack—"

"We need supplies, princess."

He knelt down and rifled through his bag. When he stood,

he held a strip of condoms—smart man—and a blue bandana.

"Just in case your fairytale requires protection," he added as he tossed the packets onto the bed.

"Or gets messy?" She nodded to the bandana.

He laughed as he sat on the edge of the bed and began to fold the blue fabric. Was he planning to break a sweat tonight?

"You can tell me no," he said. "But—"

"But I'm telling the story. You don't get to add props."

"Give this one a shot." He raised his hands and tied the bandana around his head. Then he drew it down over his eyes. He leaned back on the mattress, keeping his feet planted on the floor. "I want you to feel safe to take what you need from me. To feel what you need to feel."

She stared at the naked warrior on the bed. Her feet refused to move. Take what she needed? Safety and trust—those feelings were out of her reach. She'd lived without them for so long. How could he possibly slip them back into her life now? Moreover, how could she let him?

She walked over to the foot of the bed and moved between his legs. "This," she said as she wrapped her hand around his cock. "I want to feel you inside of me."

"Hell, yes." His hips lifted off the mattress, thrusting up into her hand. "But I want to give you—"

"A mind-blowing orgasm?" she asked before he could say *more*. She needed to draw the line at fantasy sex. She released his cock and climbed up on the bed, placing one knee on either side of his thighs. Then she reached for the condoms and tore one off the strip.

"In my story, the warrior stretches his arms over his head," she murmured as she removed the condom from the packet.

"Like this?" His powerful arms reached for the pillows.

"Yes." Holding the base of his cock with one hand, she rolled the condom on. "And keep them there."

She gathered her dress in one hand, raising it to her waist, as she positioned him at her entrance with the other hand. Slowly, she slid down, closing her eyes as her body stretched to accommodate him.

This man filled her so completely. She silently thanked him for covering his eyes. This way, he couldn't watch her staring down at him in awe. Part of her wished the story didn't have to end, that she could be the princess—and oh God, his lover.

She shifted her hips back and forth. Leaning back as far as she dared, she arched her back and placed one hand on his thigh. His cock pulsed inside her, hitting just the right spot...

"Oh, Jack," she moaned, lifting her hips up one inch and then another before sliding back down.

"I bet you're quite a sight right now," he murmured. "If I pulled off the blindfold, would I see my dick sliding in and out of you?"

"Yes," she gasped as she rode him, searching for the perfect pace. His body remained still beneath her. His abs contracted, offered a taut, hard surface for her to play.

She wanted to feel him there, inside her, but she also needed more. She released her dress and allowed the fabric to float down around her.

"Natalie," he said as his hands formed tight fists over his head.

She moved her hands to his chest and leaned forward until the part of her body that needed attention rubbed up against him. The friction inside and out pushed her up against the edge of an orgasm.

"Come with me," she said. She bit back her plea. She was so close to begging—too close.

She rocked forward. The motion spiraled beyond her control. And she chased the pleasure. Pressing her palms flat against his chest, she lifted her hips. But this time he thrust up into her.

And the pleasure caught up with her, sweeping her away into the land of "Oh, Jack!" When it subsided, she collapsed on his chest.

"What happens next?" he demanded as he wrapped his arms around her.

"Hmm?" she murmured, still aware of his hard cock buried deep inside her. She opened her eyes and studied the hard lines of his chest. She felt like Jell-O, but every inch of him remained tense. Apparently, she'd taken a solo trip to Orgasm-land. He was still ready to go.

"To the princess in your story?" His hips shifted beneath her, seeking friction. "What's next for her?"

She runs away, terrified at the thought of happily ever after with her blindfolded lover.

"I don't know," she said. "I'm not great with endings. But you still win this one. For letting me tell the story."

"It sure as hell doesn't feel like it," he growled. His hands ran over her shoulders and down to her dress. "I'm about five seconds from coming, whether you finish the damn story or not."

"Five seconds?" she said, lifting her upper body off his chest, breaking free from his touch.

"Four." His hands shifted to her thighs, gliding up her bare skin and disappearing beneath her rumpled sundress. "Three."

"Okay." She stared down at the blindfolded SEAL. His jaw was tight from holding back and the muscles in his arms bulged. And while it served him right for not letting go when she'd told him to, this was her story. He didn't get to write the ending. And looking at him now, she realized that she didn't have to send the girl riding off into the sunset with Prince Charming.

"The *girl* gave the prince exactly what he'd said he wanted," she said with a smile. She pushed his hands off her thighs and lifted her body off him, moving to his side.

"For the record," he said. "This is not what I want."

"My story." She swung her leg over him, and with her back to his chest, she lowered down onto his still-eager cock. "And then she rode him until he came screaming her name."

"Reverse cowgirl." He let out a laugh as his hands covered her ass and held on for the ride. "Hell, you are what I want darlin."

Chapter Nineteen

From his perspective—lying beneath Natalie while she rode his dick straight to heaven—throwing the bet was the second best decision he'd ever made. Using his bandana as a makeshift blindfold took first place. Without his sight, every move she made was fucking intense. And the mental picture of what she looked like right now kept him on the edge of exploding.

But he'd held back, determined to make damn sure she woke up in the morning with irrefutable proof, in the form of two "Oh Jack" orgasms, that they were good together. She would win this round. And he'd still claim the ultimate victory.

He ran his hands over her ass and gave her a squeeze. "Are you holding your dress around your waist?" he asked.

"Yes," she gasped. "And Jack, there's a mirror on the bathroom door. I'm facing it, and every time I rise up, I can see your cock. I can watch you slide into me."

Okay, that mental image started his internal clock counting down to the big O again. But he wasn't going there without her.

"Lean back," he said as he released her ass. "Let me unzip your dress."

She obeyed, still rocking her hips.

Five, four, three…

Shit, he needed to get this thing off her. His upper body curled off the bed as he fumbled his way to her zipper. He drew it down a few inches, but then the zipper stopped. Stuck.

Shit.

"Jack?"

"I'll get you a new one," he promised as he grabbed the fabric above the zipper and tore the dress open. And then, with her help, they wrestled the destroyed fabric over her head, and finally, her clothing disappeared.

"Now, tell me what you see," he said.

He waited for her words, demanding that his dick hold the fuck on and wait until she was ready to come, too.

"My breasts are bouncing," she murmured.

"Hold them." He wrapped his hands around her waist. "I've got you. You won't fall. Just place your hands on your tits."

He lifted her higher, knowing she'd see more of him. And then he lowered her slowly.

"Oh, your cock," she moaned.

Is ready to explode.

Shit, he needed her with him.

"I'm going to lift you up one more time," he said. "When I lower you back down, I need you to come. Hold your tits with one arm and reach your other hand down and touch yourself. Watch your fingers play with your—"

"Oh, wow, Jack!"

And that was all he needed to hear. He raised her up and lowered her one last time. His hips pumped up into her as he finally let go.

"Fuck!" His back arched off the bed, his hips pressing up

into her as she clamped down on the part of his body ready and willing to rename every damn orgasm from this moment on—

"Natalie!" he bellowed.

And then, slowly, the pleasure faded, leaving him with one helluva happy memory. His hands fell away from her hips. He felt her dismount and move to his side, her body stretched out on the bed. He reached up and pulled the bandana off and tossed it down to the floor.

"I don't understand," she murmured.

Me neither. But let's not question the sex gods right now.

Not that he wanted to give them credit.

"You asked for mind-blowing." He turned on his side, needing to see her now that he'd abandoned the blindfold. Her long black hair fell over her shoulders and teased her taut nipples. The rest of her body sank into the mattress, offering hope that she'd experienced an unforgettable climax.

She turned her head and looked up at him. "I don't understand how all those women who fall for your pick-up lines walk away afterward."

He raised an eyebrow, trying to hide the fact that her words felt like a knee to the groin. *All those women* did not belong in bed with him right now.

"First off, I don't have a harem stashed away somewhere," he said. "And second, I haven't gone looking for more than a night or two in a long time."

And most of the time, he didn't have to work all that hard for a chance at a naked sleepover. A smile, some eye contact in a bar, and a lousy line or two led to a pajama-less party in his bed.

But Natalie? She challenged him every step of the way. And shit, she listened to him.

"And after a night or two, you what? Leave them mourning the loss of those 'mind-blowing' orgasms?" she asked, the dazed look fading from her brown eyes.

"That good, huh?"

"You know it was," she shot back. She moved her right foot in an attempt to kick him, but he caught her thigh with his hand and drew her leg between his.

"I do." He ran his hand over her stomach, up to her breasts, and stopped with his fingers resting over her sternum. "If it's so good, why are you still pushing me away? There's no bet now. I want you, Natalie. And you know we're good together."

"Is this why you forfeited?" she demanded, the fight returning to her brown eyes as she pulled her leg free from his. "For more sex?"

She slid off the bed, demanding physical space. But that only reinforced his point. The woman he'd fantasized about for so damn long wanted him, too. And he wasn't willing to let her go without a fight.

"No." He sat up and looked her straight in the eyes. "I realized I had my eye on the wrong prize."

She laughed as she backed away from him, heading for the door. "I'm not something you can win. Another challenge that will prove to your brothers once and for all there's nothing you can't do."

"Natalie, I wanted you long before my brothers walked into your bar," he said quietly. "I didn't go after you because you didn't act as if you liked me. But then you kissed me—"

"To shut up your brothers."

He shook his head, pushed off the bed, and stood in front of her. "Not that kiss. The one in the back room of the bar. The way you responded to my touch…"

"No," she murmured.

"I should have walked away from the bet and told you that I want you more than a win. But I was looking for an excuse to get close to you. And hell, the spark in your eyes when you toss out a dare? The fire I saw when my brothers threw out that stupid challenge? I couldn't walk away from that. From you."

"You wanted a naked slumber party," she said, her gaze shifting south.

"Yes." His erection jutted out from his body, appearing eager to prove her point. "But that's not all I want. I threw the bet because I want to dream about naked slumber parties with you while I'm overseas. And then I want to come home to the real thing. To you."

*R*un.
    The word flashed in her mind like a neon warning sign. She took a step back, ready to bolt for the door—and leave behind her destroyed dress, her cell phone, and her room key. Because he wanted her?

No, she didn't need to risk security footage of her racing naked through a Vegas hotel. She needed to move the conversation back to the bedroom. Sure, he'd thrown the bet. But he still wanted that same thing.

Her.

In his bed.

Except now he wanted a chance to prove they fit. And she knew the truth. She wasn't someone's missing puzzle piece.

Are you sure? Maybe six feet plus of naked Navy SEAL is your perfect fit?

Part of her wished to take him up on his offer. She wanted to let down her guard and open herself to the possibility that maybe one day she could surrender her heart to this man.

He'll crush it.

"Natalie?"

She stared at the very aroused warrior who'd driven her

crazy for years. "I'm not looking for an endless slumber party. Tell me how you want to take me tonight. And if that's not enough for you, then I'll go."

"I'm not going to turn and walk away from you." He closed the space between them.

Temptation rose up and threatened to overwhelm her. But she held back. She didn't sink into his arms and melt at those words. They were just words. They'd traded so many since they'd left Coronado, weaving stories together.

"What do you want?" she said.

He reached for her. His hands skimmed the back of her thighs as he pulled her close and then lifted her up. She wrapped her arms around his neck, allowing him to guide her legs into position around his hips. Strong hands palmed her bottom, holding her in place.

"I want to get you wet," he growled.

"Done," she murmured, looking straight into his blue eyes. Couldn't he feel her wet and ready against his erection?

"All of you." He pivoted and carried her into the bathroom.

She looked around the space, resisting the temptation to rub up against the hard length nestled between her legs. The large, square shower stall stood in the corner, and he headed straight for it with her still wrapped around him.

He pinned her against the glass wall that separated the shower from the rest of the bathroom, holding her up with one powerful arm. He pushed the shower door open with the other, reached inside, and turned on the water.

She ran one hand down over his bicep. "Even when I was trying to ignore you while I worked and you sat across the bar, I always noticed the way your T-shirts hugged your muscles. You must have caught me looking once or twice."

"I never noticed," he said, turning her away from the shower and resting her backside on the edge of the sink. "I was too busy staring at your ass."

He claimed her mouth, his tongue sweeping past her lips and touching hers. His hands glided up her legs and pushed her thighs further apart as his lips moved over her jaw and down her neck. His touch shifted higher and higher, until he reached her breast. Then he ran his palms over her nipples.

"Jack," she gasped as she leaned back—and nearly fell into the sink.

"Reach behind you," he said, his tone rough as he released her breasts and guided her arms into position. "Hold on to the faucets."

She obeyed, placing one hand on the cold and the other on the hot. He pulled her hips forward and pressed her thighs wide, opening her body to him.

"Don't move." His gaze roamed over her as he reached for an open black bag on the counter and retrieved a condom.

"Here?" she said, feeling the muscles in her arms work to keep her from sinking into the basin.

"I can't wait for the shower to warm up." He stepped back, desire burning bright in his blue eyes as he tore open the packet and rolled the condom over his cock. "I want you like this."

She let out a laugh. "I offer you anything and you choose the bathroom sink?"

"Trust me." He moved between her legs. Hands on hips holding her steady, he thrust into her.

"Jack," she gasped.

"Hold on tight," he ordered.

"I can't." Her arms trembled, fighting to hold her up as he filled her.

"Yes, you can," he said, drawing her bottom to the edge of the vanity. Her breasts thrust into the air. He leaned over, still pumping into her, and ran his teeth over her nipple.

"I don't think I can," she cried as she tightened around

his cock. He'd pushed her so close. But she fought the orgasm. She didn't want to come. Not like this. Hovering over a sink.

He lifted his head as his hips slammed into her. "I've got you, Natalie. You're safe."

"No, I'm not," she said, raising her voice to be heard over the shower. Her thighs clenched, holding him close, daring her to stop this when it would be so easy to give in and trust him. "Please. Stop."

He pulled out of her and gently set her on the edge of the sink. His hands moved up her back, drawing her forward and out of her precarious position.

"I'm sorry," she said as she released the faucets. "But I couldn't—"

And that was a lie. She'd been on the verge of the promised mind-blowing orgasm—while completely at his mercy. He'd claimed control, calling the shots—and she'd liked it.

She closed her eyes, picturing the way she looked, her body open to him, with her hands behind her. A soft moan escaped. Oh God, she wanted to let him take her just like that, to believe that he'd keep her safe. But to offer her trust?

"Shh, I've got you," he said, lifting her off the vanity. Her feet touched the floor, but he kept one arm around her, holding her steady. He reached his free hand between them and ran his fingers over her clit. "Trust me, Natalie."

She leaned her head against his shoulder. Her arms remained at her sides as he touched her. His finger moved quickly, hitting the right spots with the perfect amount of pressure. It was as if he'd memorized a roadmap of her body.

"Jack." His name sounded like a plea, like he'd finally reduced her to begging. Her body stiffened. He flicked her clit one last time. "Jack!"

She pulled away, stumbling back. But it was too late. The orgasm she'd begged for swept over her with all the subtlety of a freight train.

"Oh God." She moved away until she felt the vanity at her back. Her fingers curled around the counter's edge. "Jack." And finally—*finally*—it faded. She opened her eyes. "I'm sorry, but I can't do this. Without the bet—"

"You need an excuse to be with me," he said, his voice sharp and so far from charming that she took a step back. He crossed his arms in front of his chest, his muscles—from his biceps to his condom-covered erection—tense. He looked like a warrior ready to pounce. "Admit it. If you take the bet and my stupid-ass brothers out of the equation, you would have to face the possibility that you want to be with me. You'd have to trust me."

"I can't," she said quickly. She saw the flash of hurt in his blue eyes. Her words hurt. He might not admit it, but she knew him. Jack Barnes had spent his childhood straight through his years with the SEALs trying to prove he was good enough. And she'd handed him proof. "It's not you," she added. "I can't let you in."

Please let him understand.

"Helluva time to play the 'it's not you, it's me' card," he snapped.

She took another step back. "I can't give you what you want."

"I want you in my shower."

"And after that?" she said. She knew the happiness would fade and break apart. It wouldn't last.

He stared at her as he drew a deep breath. "I want you. No bets. No escape routes. Just you."

"No." She released the counter and moved to the door, her back to the suite behind her. She kept her gaze locked on Jack, the man who wanted so much more than she could give. "I can't fall for you. If I do…"

She shook her head.

"Natalie." He reached for her. His fingers curled around

her bicep. And for a second, she feared he'd hold her here and force her to face a future that would lead to heartbreak.

"Let me go. *Now*." She pulled free from his grasp. Then, she turned away and rushed out of the bathroom.

"Wait. Please—"

But she kept going. She scanned his bedroom—and her torn dress—grabbed the white button-down shirt he'd stripped off three orgasms ago and pulled it on.

"When you start measuring time by orgasms," she murmured as she grabbed her cell off the floor and headed for the door. "It is definitely time to end the naked slumber party."

A future filled with pleasure, happiness, and heaven help her, Jack—that was too good to be true. She'd had a taste of happiness, a taste of him, and she couldn't risk another.

Chapter Twenty

The hotel room door slammed, stealing away Jack's chance to turn his long-standing fantasy into reality—Natalie in his life and his bed, night after night.

He stood in the middle of his hotel bathroom, the shower raining down behind him. His condom-wrapped dick jutted out from his body, still eager for a future that was never going to happen.

Should he go after her? He stepped toward the bathroom door and froze. What the hell could he say that he hadn't already put out there? He'd made it clear that he'd wanted her long before the bet. Maybe he could chase her down the hall and explain.

His jaw tightened. He could guess at her response. *Don't play Prince Charming with me.*

No, he was done playing "Prince Charming." He'd said everything he had to say.

I want you, Natalie. No bets. No escape routes. Just you.

What else could he possibly say to keep her?

Nothing.

He opened the shower door and stepped back under the warm water. He closed his eyes and tipped his head back. He'd fought for so long—against his brothers, against everyone who doubted he had what it took to become a SEAL, and against fucking terrorists hell-bent on destroying everything he believed in, like his country and his freedom. But this was one battle he couldn't win.

Because Natalie wasn't a prize.

When she said those words—shit, he'd known she was right. And he should have listened to her. He should have demanded clothes and conversation, not a quick fuck in a hotel bathroom. This wasn't about who came out on top. And if she'd stop running and think about it for a minute, she'd realize this thing between them wasn't about who set the scene in bed.

Tell me how you want to take me.

His body ached at the memory of those words on her lips. He had a list to complete that would take them months, maybe years given his near-constant deployments. But he'd blown his chances of ever making that happen. Natalie had made it clear she didn't want him.

And her rejection hurt more than every damn hit he'd taken as a kid. More than his brothers' ugly words. More than anything he'd faced during his time with the SEAL teams.

They were done. She'd left him alone.

Damn, he wanted to escape the pain.

Leaning forward, he pressed one hand against the shower wall. He wrapped the other around his dick and stripped off the condom. He sure as hell didn't need it for this. He pumped his hand up and down. The mental image of Natalie on the counter, her arms behind her, breasts jutting out and her legs spread. He'd never forget how she looked at that moment. And how damn much he wanted to take her and make her *his*.

"It's a fucking fantasy," he said, water rushing over his back as his hand worked faster. He didn't need to draw this out, not when he was alone in the shower.

He closed his eyes and came, releasing a moan. It felt good, sure. But right now he'd take a simple conversation with the one woman who listened, who understood how the past drove him to make stupid calls—like the bet. He'd set out to claim her on his terms. And he'd fucking failed. He sure as shit wasn't going to figure out how to fix this mess while self-gratifying in the shower.

"*If* I can fix this," he muttered, opening his eyes and staring out into the empty bathroom. Maybe defeat had finally caught up with him. He could beat his brothers. He could take down terrorists. But making the woman of his dreams open up her heart and take a chance on him?

Fucking impossible. He should go back to sitting on his side of the bar and tossing out stupid one-liners to women who didn't give a damn what he said as long as he smiled.

Any minute security would turn the corner and demand to know what she was doing running down the hall in a barely buttoned men's shirt with her cell phone pressed against her ear.

Please pick up, Cade. I promise I won't complain about the fact that Mufasa spends most of his time with me when he's really your dog. Please. I need you now.

"Natalie?"

"What's your room number?" she demanded, praying his suite was on the same floor as Jack's room.

"One nine zero five," he said.

"Nineteenth floor. Oh thank God." She slowed and looked at the sign by the elevator bank. She was so close, only one more stretch of hopefully empty hallway to run down without her underwear.

"Do you need help with Mufasa?" he asked.

"No, your dog—"

"Our dog," he corrected.

"Mufasa is fine." She stopped in front of room nineteen zero five. "I need you, Cade. And I'm outside your room."

The door swung open as she lowered her phone from her ear. Her best friend, and her only hope for surviving this night that was sliding so far out of her control, filled the entryway. He was wearing boxers and an inside out T-shirt, but he was still overdressed compared to her.

"What the hell?" he said, his eyes widening. But he didn't hesitate. He stepped back, holding the door wide open. "Get in here."

"Is Lucia—"

"She's here." He closed the door, turned the lock, and moved into the room. He kept his gaze fixed on the floor.

"Natalie?" Her sister stood by the bed securing a bathrobe tie around her waist. "What happened?"

Cade bypassed her and headed for the bathroom. He returned with a white hotel robe that matched her sister's.

"Here." Cade held out the oversize robe. "Put this on."

"Thank you." She set her phone on the floor and pulled the soft fabric over her half-buttoned shirt.

"Now sit down." He made the command sound like an invitation. With Cade, it was always a request spoken in his deep voice. Unlike Jack—

"Tell us why you're running through the hotel in Jack's shirt." He claimed one of the armchairs in the sitting area that was an exact replica of the space in Jack's room, and he motioned for her to take the other. "And nothing else."

And now it was her turn to dissect the carpet pattern, her gaze fixed on the floor.

Deep breaths. No tears. Cade will understand.

He'd run fast and hard from commitment for so long. For years, they'd had their own club of sorts.

"Natalie, if he hurt you—" The big, bad Navy SEAL's voice shook.

"If who hurt her?" Lucia demanded, crossing to the sitting area. She placed her hands on her hips. "Is this about Jack? Why would he hurt her?"

"I'll tear him apart," Cade continued as though he hadn't heard his fiancé. "I don't care if it lands me in a Vegas jail the night before my wedding."

She looked up. Her best friend sat on the edge of his chair, forearms resting on his thighs. His expression was a mask of concern. And her sister—Lucia looked like a furious angel in her white robe.

"He didn't hurt me," Natalie said.

Liar. Jack Barnes had taken a jackhammer to her defenses, breaking down the walls around her heart. And she was so afraid he'd fought his way in.

"Then where are your clothes?" Lucia asked.

"I was in a rush—"

"To get away from him." Cade clenched his jaw and shook his head. "Look, I've been trying not to get involved in your bet. But I know Jack. He doesn't give up. I know he admitted defeat. But if he made one more play—"

"He won the bet," she said softly.

"I'll fucking kill him." Cade was on his feet, his hands balled into fists at his side.

"Bet?" Lucia said, her sharp gaze moving between her fiancé and Natalie.

"Don't blame Jack," she said, looking Cade straight in the eyes. "I wanted him. After the bachelorette party yesterday, I gave in. I let him win. And then today he told his team that he was giving up and—"

"What. Bet." Lucia spoke loud and clear over their rapid-fire conversation.

Oh shit.

"You said you would tell her," Cade said.

"Someone better tell me now," Lucia demanded.

"Earlier this week, before we left for Vegas…" Natalie began. She told her sister about Colton's challenge, how she'd overheard, and how she'd sworn Jack would never win. "I planned to tell you," she added. "After the wedding. After Jack lost. Only he didn't lose…"

And I'm terrified I'm falling for him.

Only she couldn't say those last words to her best friend and sister—two people who'd found love and fought for it.

"Cade." Lucia turned to her fiancé. "Maybe you should visit your dog. Natalie and I need girl time."

Her sister turned to her, and Natalie braced for a rush of angry words. They'd just started to rebuild their relationship, and she'd kept a secret from her sister—one that was blowing up the night before Lucia's wedding.

Natalie closed her eyes. When was she going to stop messing up her little sister's life? Ever since their parents had died, she'd managed to rain chaos and pain on her little sister. This was exactly why she'd kept her distance from Lucia for so long.

But Lucia didn't yell at her, or turn into Bridezilla. Her sister waited until her fiancé picked up his phone and the stack of room keys. She remained silent while Cade kissed her long and hard on the lips before slipping into the hall.

Then Lucia turned to her, her eyes shining with determination. "We're going to fix this, Natalie."

Impossible.

But one question chased that thought like a cool drink of water following a shot of burning whiskey.

"How?" she murmured. "I ran away, left him in the middle

of… It wasn't a good time to go. And I took his shirt."

The phone's shrill ring was like an alarm bell punctuating the rising panic in her voice. Lucia walked to the nightstand and answered it.

"Yes, she's here with me. Cade went to look after his dog," she said, her words tight and sharp. "You might want to wait and return her clothes in the morning."

Jack.

Of course, any man with half a brain would call around to make sure the woman who'd raced out of his room half-dressed was all right. And Jack wasn't stupid. Not by a long shot.

Her sister hung up the phone and crossed the suite to the sitting area.

"Lucia, I'm sorry—"

"I'm sorry Cade's stupid teammate bet he could sleep with you." Lucia sank into the chair across from her. "But if he hadn't, you'd probably have ignored him while he fought for your attention."

"I think that would have been better than this," she muttered. The chaos. The fear. "I ran down the hallway without my underwear."

"What happened? Why did you leave in the middle…" Her sister waved her hand in the air.

"I gave myself one more night with him." She closed her eyes. "But then we…in his bathroom…the shower was running, and I was so close to saying, 'Yes, I trust you.'"

Lucia's brow furrowed. "And that's a bad thing? He's a good guy, Natalie. The bet was stupid. But we all have our Achilles' heel. I'm guessing Jack's brothers are his weak spot. That doesn't mean you can't trust him. Cade trusts him to cover his back while they're off fighting who knows where."

"I know." Natalie had faith that he'd keep her safe. But this went beyond his physical demands. She trusted him not to hurt her while she had her arms behind her back and her body hovered over the bathroom sink. But—

"I don't trust him with my heart." There. She'd put the massive roadblock into words. She could give up physical control and admit that she liked it when he gave orders in bed. But she couldn't give him free rein to trample her emotions. When he said those words—trust me—she'd known that she needed to escape.

"Did he ask you to hand it over?" Lucia asked.

"This isn't just sex for the sake of winning a bet, or even for the sake of sex. Not anymore. I care too much. And I think he might feel the same way. He lost that bet for me, Lucia. He wanted me more."

Lucia smiled. "I know it's scary, falling for a gorgeous warrior determined to prove he wants a place in your life—trust me, I've been there. But when the alternative is walking away from the person you love? From a future where the good outweighs all the bad—past and present—simply because that person is a part of your life? I think the odds are in your favor."

She shook her head as tears trailed down her cheeks. "Not for me. Good things don't happen to me. Our parents died in a car crash. Two foster families sent us back. Because of me. And the third—"

"What happened to me was not your fault. If you had been there…" Lucia drew a long shaky breath. "If you had been there, the bastard might have gone after you."

"I know." She spent years wishing she'd stayed home, that she'd drawn his anger away from Lucia. "I should have been there that night."

"No!" Lucia was on her feet the minute the words slipped out, crossing the sitting area and drawing her up into her arms. "I hate what that man did to me. But I have never blamed you. Not once. You were there for me. Always. Even in some of the darkest moments, you were my good thing."

Tears ran down Natalie's face, and she clung to her sister. "But I barely got to see you. When you were in the hospital, and then after…"

Lucia drew back and met her teary-eyed gaze. "But even when I was lost in pain and anger, I knew I had a sister who loved me, who would jump to my defense, even going as far as sending her best friend to play bodyguard. I'm just sorry I haven't been here for you. You deserve the love of a good man, Natalie. You deserve a SEAL."

"But what if—"

"Shh." Lucia pressed a finger to her lips. "Stop waiting for the sky to fall."

She pulled free from her sister's embrace and wrapped her arms around her waist. "I'm not sure it's Jack. He…he pushes me out of my comfort zone."

And yes, she'd chosen those words carefully. She was not about to discuss sexual positions or kinks with the little sister she was just getting to know—or anyone else. Not even Cade. He knew her better than anyone on the planet. But there were some lines they didn't cross.

Lucia laughed, her eyes, damp from tears, sparkling. "Cade did the same thing. And it was the best thing that ever happened to me."

"What if I try and it doesn't work?" she said softly.

"You've still won," Lucia said firmly. "Because you gave the relationship a shot. And I bet you'll succeed. I've never known you to back down from anything."

"Just what I need, another bet," Natalie murmured.

"Even if he breaks your heart," Lucia continued, clearly pretending she hadn't heard her. "You've got us. I'll be there to help you pick up the pieces. I promise. And so will Cade. This time, if it all goes to hell, you won't be alone."

"You'll have your hands full with your family." Natalie

nodded to her sister's stomach.

"You are my family," Lucia said firmly. "If he hurts you, I'll be there. And Cade will kick his ass."

She closed her eyes. If she took the risk and the cloud of doom that seemingly hung over her life let loose a hailstorm, she wouldn't be alone. That was something. But was it enough to say *I trust you* to the Prince Charming of Navy SEALs?

Chapter Twenty-One

J ack routinely operated on very little sleep knowing that someone would be waiting to kick his ass at sunrise. But today was different. He planned to let his opponent win. And he'd come bearing gifts for the man who'd likely throw a punch or two first, and then ask about the bakery box.

He stepped off the elevator and found Cade staring out the lobby window with his hands in the pockets of his cargo shorts. "Hey man, about last night," he said when he reached his teammate. "I messed up. I should have insisted on a real, honest conversation with Natalie before the clothes came off and—"

"You should stop right there and open the box," Cade said.

Jack flipped the white lid off and revealed a dozen doughnuts. Boston cream. Powdered sugar. Glazed. Chocolate. He'd listened to his teammate bitch about the lack of doughnuts when visiting the world's terrorist hot spots and knew this was his best chance at placating Cade before he started throwing punches on his wedding day.

Cade selected a chocolate glazed. "You do realize that you'd have a better shot at talking to Natalie if you showed up at *her* door with doughnuts."

Jack shook his head. "I won't be showing up at her door again. You have my word on that. Natalie made it clear that she's done."

"You're giving up?" Cade headed for the front doors to the hotel.

"I'm not going to stalk your girl. The bet was bad enough."

"Yeah."

Jack followed his teammate out to the valet area where Cade's Jeep stood. He glanced at his teammate. "Having second thoughts?"

Forget his problems. Shit, this was serious. If Cade was having cold feet, rethinking his trip to the altar…

"No, but the waiting is driving me insane. So Red Rock Canyon, here we come. Time for a little physical training." Cade climbed into the driver's side, set the doughnut on the dash, and turned the key.

"PT before your wedding night?" Jack watched the hotel disappear from sight as they drove down the famous Strip.

"I'll have time for a nap. Who the hell thought a four o'clock ceremony was a good idea? We've been in Vegas for days now. I should have taken her to the nearest chapel the minute we hit the Strip on Thursday. We could have spent the weekend celebrating as husband and wife."

"I thought Lucia wanted the real deal," Jack said, still stumbling through relief. Cade wasn't looking to hightail it back to Coronado. Thank you, Jesus.

"She does," the groom confirmed. "Flowers. The dress. A hairstyle that will take three damn hours. And I want her to have it all."

Jack nodded. He opened the bakery box resting on his lap and selected a glazed doughnut. They drove in silence as Cade merged onto the highway out of town.

"You can't give up on Natalie because she got scared and

ran," Cade said.

Jack groaned and closed his eyes. "You're taking me to the desert to fucking lecture me?"

"Natalie's not going to hand over her trust after a night or two," Cade continued. "And it has nothing to do with the bet. She doesn't let people in because she's afraid the sky will fucking fall if she does. She expects the worst. Natalie sees a future with you as impossible for her."

"Impossible," Jack said. He wanted to tackle the challenge and win. But this wasn't a war. He couldn't win simply by digging his heels in and refusing to give up. "Yeah, well, that sums it up, doesn't it? Yet you think I should show up with doughnuts and set myself up to take a second hit when Natalie has made it clear she always planned to go back to ignoring me. I don't think so."

"She's had a lot of people ripped from her life," Cade said quietly. "She's learned to save herself the pain by not letting anyone in."

"I don't want in," Jack said firmly.

"Bullshit." He took his eyes off the road for a second and glared at him.

"Let it go, Cade. I can't make her love me."

His teammate nodded and they drove in silence. Jack glanced out the window at the wide-open desert. "Where is Red Rock Canyon?"

"About twenty miles from the Strip. We're getting close."

To the middle of nowhere.

"I have the wedding rings hidden in my room," Jack said. "Might be hard to find them if you leave me out here."

"Thought about it last night," Cade admitted as he turned and steered the Jeep into a parking area. A handful of cars were lined by the trailhead, including a pickup that looked exactly like Dante's truck. Jack scanned the area. There it was—visual confirmation. The truck belonged to their recently divorced

SEAL. And it looked like he'd abandoned his role as fake orgasm spectator in favor of audience participation in the real deal.

"What the…?" Cade said, turning the key. "Was that…?"

Yeah, Jack wasn't the only one who'd caught an eyeful of their shirtless teammate following a topless woman with bright pink hair behind a large rock.

"I don't think Dante came out here to watch another fake climax," Jack said.

"We should have eloped." Cade shook his head. "Bringing a bunch of SEALS on leave to Sin City—what the hell was I thinking?"

"Let's get this over with so you can marry Lucia and we can all go home," Jack said, climbing down from the truck.

Cade reached behind his seat and pulled out two water bottles. He tossed one to Jack. "One more question."

"I don't think so." Jack headed for the trailhead.

Cade followed him. "I know you care about her, Jack. But do you love her?"

Yes.

But Jack sure as shit wasn't going to pour his heart out on the man's wedding day. He wasn't going to stand here in the desert and admit he'd lost when it came to the thing that mattered most—the woman he loved.

"Let's fucking hike." Jack picked up his pace, his jaw tight and every muscle in his body tense. "First one to that canyon wins." He nodded to a peak in the distance.

"You're on." Cade stepped off the path and moved around his teammate. "And Jack, I know you think it's over, but you should tell her."

Jack shook his head and started to run for the canyon. "First one to the canyon and back wins. I don't want to walk back listening to you go on and on above love."

Two months after her first shift at Bottom's Up, Natalie had stepped in front of a drunken sailor, a young man who had just flunked the SEAL's rigorous training camp and hated the world, including the not so intoxicated soon-to-be SEAL who'd succeeded. For a second, she'd thought the drunken sailor would hit her instead. While he'd failed BUD/S training, the man was built like a tank.

But he'd lowered his fist and allowed her to call him a cab. And in the process, he'd cemented her reputation as the bartender who could take on anyone and anything.

Including an early morning trip to a Sin City sex toy store.

"When you said we needed to take a detour on the way to the hair salon, I thought you meant coffee," Lucia said. "Or maybe a grocery store for champagne and sparkling cider, something to drink while we get ready for my walk down the aisle."

"This won't take long." Natalie stared up at the Sizzling Secrets sign and waited for the lights to blink on. She could see a salesperson moving around inside. It wouldn't be long now. "But if I'm going to try to fix things with Jack, I need to do this. I ran away from him in the middle of wild, crazy bathroom sex."

"If you're sure sex toys will fix your relationship—"

"It's not a relationship," Natalie insisted. "Not yet."

And please don't jinx it.

That was the last thing she needed.

Lucia took her hand and stood by her side, staring up at the unlit sign. "I hope you know what you're getting."

"I do."

"Good, because we need to get to hair and makeup soon. We're both walking down the aisle in a few hours."

"While I wear one very terrible tutu," Natalie said with a

sigh. "Jack might take one look at me and run away. I'll never get a chance to show him my toys."

"You're not wearing the pink dress." Her sister squeezed her hand. "I was planning to tell you later, do a big reveal in the bridal suite. I found an elegant and sexy maid-of-honor gown for you. In charcoal, not pink. The skirt is floor length and it has these long bands of fabric that cover your chest, tie at the back of your neck and then twist together to form a long rope down your back before wrapping around your waist. And if you don't like the twisted fabric down your back, there are half a dozen other ways to wear it."

Natalie stared at her sister. No Terrible Tutu. An elegant gown. "So you're saying I don't need to be here, waiting for the sex store to open? I could let Jack tie me up in my dress?"

"I'm saying that I love you. We both did what we needed to do to survive after the crash. But it's behind us. And I'm getting *married* today. In a few hours. If we make it to the salon."

Natalie glanced at the storefront. The lights in the Sizzling Secrets sign flicked on. Could she put the past behind her and have a relationship with a man who just might battle her for control every step of the way?

"Thank you for the dress. After your honeymoon, I'll invite you over and we can burn the Terrible Tutu together." Natalie drew her sister through the open door. "And in five minutes, I promise to take you to the salon. But right now, I need to find out if Sizzling Secrets carries black silk bondage ties. Because I'm going for it. I'm trying for a second chance with Jack. Something real, not based on a bet."

Lucia laughed as they bypassed vibrators. "I never would have guessed that bondage was the way to Jack's heart."

This was only one piece of the puzzle. But she was determined to show Jack that he'd been right—they fit together. And even if it frightened her, she wasn't going to walk away this time. *If* he let her back into his life and his bed.

Chapter Twenty-Two

Natalie walked through the empty courtyard that separated the hotel's main building from the Roman-style outdoor wedding venue. She cursed her shoes with each step. It was impossible to run in heels. And Lucia was waiting for her on the other side of the decorative columns along with the wedding guests. Her sister was ready to walk down the aisle and meet her groom. Or she would be ready once Natalie returned with her sister's bridal bouquet.

"She's probably the only bride to leave her flowers in the bathroom before the wedding ceremony," she muttered, pausing to shift her grip on the cascade of roses. With a firm grip on the bouquet she stepped forward—then stopped when she heard Jack's voice.

"Colton, it's over."

Jack's voice had the power to tease, to command, and right now, to stop her dead in her tracks. She moved behind one of the pillars dividing the empty courtyard from where the guests had gathered and pressed her virtually bare back—minus one twisted length of charcoal fabric—against a fake column.

She held her breath. Five minutes, probably less, until Lucia walked down the aisle and the best man was on a call with Mr. Belt Buckle?

"Listen to the message I left for you," Jack snapped. "The bet is over. And fuck you, I'm not giving you any details."

He was giving in, pretending he'd lost to the family who'd bullied him. He'd broken free from the past that had held on too tight. And if he could do it, there was hope for her—bright, beautiful hope for one more night with the charming SEAL. And one night might lead to another and another.

She glanced around the column. Chief Jack Barnes in a black tie tuxedo…wow. One look and dragging the bride into a sex toy store on her wedding day seemed like the best decision Natalie had ever made. He could stop traffic while wearing cargo pants and his signature smile. But dressed in formal wear? He'd cause a riot.

Jack could have his pick of the beautiful women who waltzed into her bar looking for a SEAL. But last night, he'd told her that he wanted her.

She drew back and pressed against the column. It still felt too good to be true—like disaster and heartache lay just around the corner. But she'd never know if she didn't try. And this time, if she stumbled into hurt and rejection, Lucia would be there to catch her. She was done living with the guilt from the past holding her back.

"Colton, I'm done," Jack said, his tone deathly serious. "I failed. Are you happy?"

There was a pause, and Natalie didn't make a sound.

"I'll send you the money," Jack snapped.

Natalie closed her eyes but stopped short of resting her head against the mock pillar. The hair stylist had gone to a lot of trouble to twist Natalie's straight black hair into a fancy updo.

She stepped forward and let Jack see her. He looked her up and down, and the glimpse of pain in his eyes made her regret every second she'd hesitated to let him know how much she wanted him.

"Enjoy that?" he said. His tone had transitioned from 'fuck you Colton,' but there was still a hard edge.

"You didn't lose, Jack."

He arched an eyebrow. "Didn't I?"

You still have me.

If he wanted her.

The string quartet sprang to life. They were literally minutes away from the ceremony. She needed to find Lucia and hand over the flowers. She couldn't ruin her sister's day. But this wasn't how she wanted to tell him, in rushed words before the wedding.

"Jack—"

"You need space. I get it, Natalie. When we get back to Coronado, I promise to stay on my side of the bar."

He turned and walked away. He moved quickly, and then he disappeared around a column. And he didn't look back. Not once.

Oh God, what if I'm too late?

He'd admitted his loss to his brothers, opening himself to endless teasing. Even though he'd won the bet. A man who would do that for her...he was worth the risk. But what if black silk ties weren't enough to convince him to give her a second chance?

*T*he things he could do to her in that dress.
     Jack kept his eyes fixed on the rope-like fabric running down Natalie's bare back. Her shoulders down to her waist offered a valley of smooth skin. And the floor-length

skirt pressed up against her legs as the groom swung her out of view.

He should be focused on Cade's advice. He should tell her that he'd fallen for her so long ago that it had hurt so damn much when she'd pushed him away as if a night or two was enough. Because even if he spent 365 days a year by her side, he would never get enough of her.

"Cade won't mind if you cut in." The bride stopped by his side.

"Thank you," he said, his gaze fixed on where Cade's hand touched Natalie's lower back. "But I'm not much of a dancer."

Lucia nodded. "That dress is perfect for her, don't you think?"

"Yes." He looked away and spotted Ronan by the bar. "I should—"

"So functional," Lucia continued, ignoring his words. "With those long lengths of fabric."

And this time he stole a quick glance at the bride. Lucia wore a curve-hugging gown that proved his teammate was a damn lucky man. His teammate should be thanking his lucky stars that he waited for the real deal versus a quickie Vegas wedding. Jack looked at her long enough to see amusement sparkling in her eyes.

"Functional." He glanced back at Natalie as a mental picture formed in his mind. Her wrists bound by the gray length currently wrapped around her waist. The long skirt pushed to her hips. His teeth drawing aside her panties...

"Excuse me," he said and turned away from Cade's gorgeous bride. He needed to get out of here before his imagination drove him crazy with crystal-clear fantasies featuring the woman he couldn't have, the one who'd run away from him, from happiness, from any hope of a future.

He stopped by the bar. He held up his empty beer and

signaled for another. Ronan was deep in conversation with Cade's father, so Jack stood to the side. Alone. And drank.

"Jack."

He turned and spotted Natalie heading straight for him wearing the expression she generally reserved for unruly sailors at Bottom's Up. The dress flowed around her and her eyes shone with determination.

So damn beautiful.

She stopped in front of him with her chin held high. "We have one more night on the same side of the bar."

"One more night," he repeated. He allowed his gaze to drift to the bands of fabric covering her breasts and disappearing behind her neck. "It's not enough," he added. He refused to be her one-night escape. Not after she'd pushed him away, sending a loud and clear signal that he wasn't enough for her.

"But it's a start," she said, her dark eyes locked with his, her gaze so bold and unwavering that his body responded and sent blood rushing south. "I dare you to join me in my room."

He set his beer on the bar. The woman he'd dreamed about for years, wrapped in a dress designed to torture him, had invited him to her bed. They might not make it beyond the entryway, but still, he couldn't walk away from her offer.

Except she'd walked out on him once and it had hurt like hell. He didn't want to retrace his steps down that path.

"How do you see this ending, Natalie?" he asked softly.

"Happy. I hope." She ran her palms down her sides, smoothing the dress over her thighs. One glance and he saw her hands tremble from nerves. She could take on a room full of brawling sailors and soldiers, but fighting for her own happiness scared the shit out of her.

Cade's words had been running through his head like a neon leaderboard since their hike.

She doesn't let people in because she's afraid the sky will fucking fall if she does. She expects the worst. Natalie sees a future with you as impossible for her.

And now she was here, asking him to take a chance on her. To take a chance on them. There was a chance it would end the same way as before. A moment of pleasure, and then she'd walk away from him again. But he'd seen soldiers in the field claim victory because they found courage when it mattered most, and he'd never forgive himself if he didn't give Natalie that same opportunity.

"You're on." He reached out and took her shaking hand, ready to follow her down a path labeled happily ever after. God help him if the signs were mislabeled and they were headed for a clusterfuck. "Darlin', I accept your dare."

Chapter Twenty-Three

Holding her skirt with one hand and the Sizzling Secrets bag with the other, she surveyed her hotel room one last time. She'd asked Jack for a few minutes to "freshen up" and he'd agreed to wait in the hall, buying her time to set the scene. Now, she was ready to reach for a future with Jack—if she wasn't too late.

He'd accepted the dare. That was a step in the right direction, wasn't it?

She placed her hand on the knob and drew a deep breath. She could do this. She could open the door and hand the charming SEAL a bag of black silk ties and say "take me." That wasn't hard. And this time, when he stripped away her physical control, she would face her fears head on and win.

She cracked the door and peered through the narrow opening. She kept the bag behind her back. He'd stripped off his black bowtie. But he looked close to perfect, standing there with his white tuxedo shirt open at the neck.

"Planning to let me in?" he asked. "If we're taking this dare into the hall, I'm warning you now, there are security cameras."

"No cameras," she said. "I need you to close your eyes."

He raised an eyebrow, but then he followed her request.

She drew a deep breath. It was now or never. She took his hand and led him into the room.

"You can open your eyes now," she said.

He obeyed, and she watched as he surveyed the suite. Rose petals covered the bed. She'd taken the time to fold the blankets down, leaving the crisp white sheets littered with red petals. A bottle of champagne rested in a bucket on the nightstand. And a pair of flutes stood beside it.

His gaze shifted to the carpet where she'd created a path of long-stem roses leading to the bed. Every detail screamed romance. And oh God, maybe it was too much. But she'd wanted to show him that she was looking beyond tonight. He could bind her to the bed and she'd still be here in the morning.

He turned to her. "You've been planning this dare?"

"Yes." She held out the Sizzling Secrets bag. "I went shopping before the wedding."

He took the bag. With one handle in each hand, he opened it but kept his eyes on her. "May I?" he asked.

She nodded.

He withdrew the four lengths of black silk and glanced up at her. "You intended to seduce me with romance and bondage?"

"Yes." She met his intense gaze briefly. Then she turned her attention to the ties in his hands. Had she made a mistake? She'd asked the store clerk to modify them, trimming off the silver rings at the end until they looked like the ones from his story.

"Natalie."

She looked up at him, hoping for a hint of his give-me-your-panties grin. But his mouth formed a thin line as he studied her.

"What if I want to be more than the guy who ties you up?"

Her hope threatened to leap off a cliff. She glanced at the ties in his hand and her brow furrowed. "But I thought you wanted—"

"Not tonight." He draped the black silk lengths over the back of the desk chair. "We'll set these here." Then he turned to her. "Tonight, I was hoping you'd tell me what you like."

You. On top of me. Inside me. Pushing my boundaries and daring me to leave the past behind...

She stole a glance at the discarded ties. She'd planned to follow his lead and obey his commands tonight. Now, she felt like she'd stepped onto thin ice. Any moment, the surface might break and she'd lose him—for good this time.

"I'd like to know if you're wearing underwear," she said, reaching for light and playful.

"I'm not," he said. And for the first time tonight, she detected a note of humor threaded with desire in his tone. Her hope soared.

You can do this. You can fight for happiness.

"Prove it." She lowered her gaze to his crotch. She would seduce him tonight with or without the ties. She would not run away and hide. "Take off your clothes, Jack."

He reached for the top button on his shirt. "What about you? Are you wearing panties under that dress?"

She followed his example, her fingers moving to the complex knot at her back. Once she loosened it, the twisted length running up her back would unravel, and the bands of fabric would fall off her shoulders and reveal her breasts.

"Don't take off all of your clothes just yet," he said. "I've spent the entire reception dreaming about you in that dress, my hands sliding under that rope at your back."

She lowered her hands and waited for his command.

Finally, she felt as if she'd stepped onto solid ground. This worked—him calling the shots one moment before handing the reins back to her.

This is why we fit. But what if he doesn't see it?

"That doesn't mean you can't show me what you're wearing underneath," he said, pulling his tuxedo shirt free from his pants. He stripped it off and let it fall to the floor. "Lift your dress and show me."

Desire ripped through her. She buried her fingers in the soft material by her thighs. Her fingers drew her dress higher and higher, revealing her legs inch by inch. He followed her hemline, barely blinking as he kicked off his shiny black shoes. By the time she reached her thighs, he'd slid his pants down his legs.

Jack Barnes could start a riot in a tux. But naked? She'd have to be crazy to walk away from that body. Add in the fact that man attached to that long, hard cock still wanted her after seeing her nearly crippling fears on display? After she'd run from him? And oh yes, she'd be bat-shit crazy to walk away again.

"Higher, Natalie," he growled. His hands remained at his side.

She kept her movements slow and steady. She wanted to draw this out, but she could feel herself growing wet. She stole another glance at his long, hard length, then down his powerful legs. He stood with his feet planted hips distance apart. And he looked ready to pounce.

On her.

"You're killing me, darlin'," he said. "And if that's what you want, I'm in. But know that I'm about five seconds away from falling to my knees and begging to see you."

She gathered her skirt at her waist and offered him a clear view of her white lace thong—from the front.

"But I know you've always liked the view from the back,"

she said, turning around.

"Sweet Jesus," he murmured.

She glanced over her shoulder and watched as he stared at the thin strip of white lace disappearing between her naked cheeks. "A little different from at the bar?"

"Tell me what you want, Natalie," he said, his tone wavering between begging and demanding. He stared at her, his blue eyes roaming over her body. And she knew he was waiting for her to offer more—beyond the rose petals and silk ties.

"I want to star in your story."

Chapter Twenty-Four

Jack focused on her words—*I want to star in your story*. He was determined to prove that he could be more than the guy who offered bondage-filled fantasies, more than her friend and sometimes-lover. And shit, he was determined to win the head-to-head battle with that dress.

Seeing the full skirt bunched around her waist, knowing he could unravel the material at her waist, loosen the rope at her back, and use her clothes to tie her to the bed...

But not tonight. Right now he needed to feel her trust here in the room with them giving life to their future. One day, they'd use her dress, and maybe the black silk ties she brought.

He stole a quick glance at her purchase from Sizzling Secrets. When he'd introduced the fantasy, he'd reached for a mental picture that would turn them on. And he'd freaking loved the way she responded to his words. But the fact that she'd listened and gone out of her way to transform a piece of his fantasy into a very real possibility? He hoped like hell that was a sign they'd steered clear of clusterfuck territory.

"Jack?"

He looked back at her and watched as she widened her stance. God help him if she bent over.

"I want my story," she said, her voice so damn sexy.

He drew a deep breath. "How to F… How to Make Love to—"

"You can say fuck, Jack," she said with a soft laugh.

"How to Fuck a Princess." He stepped over the roses and moved behind her. His dick pressed against her as his hands slipped under her raised dress. "Part One."

"It's part of a series?" she asked, leaning into him.

"Yes." He toyed with the elastic band of her underwear before hooking his thumbs underneath and slowly drawing the slip of white lace down her legs. He knelt by her ankles and said, "Step out."

"How many parts?" she asked, lifting first one foot and then the other. "Sometimes it is nice to know before you start a series when you'll reach the conclusion."

"This one could go on for a long time," he admitted, tossing her underwear aside. He stood and reached for her, running his hands over her bare skin to the knotted material at the back of her dress. "I don't have an ending planned."

"That's good," she murmured. "I recently realized I have an irrational fear of endings."

His hands froze on her dress. "Still expecting the worst?"

She drew a shaky breath. "Not this time. It's possible. But I'm trying to focus on the good parts."

"Good." Relief rushed in and his fingers started to move again.

"Jack, how does your story start?"

"Once upon a time, there was a prince." He loosened the knot, and holding one piece in each hand, began to unwind the twisted fabric running up her back.

"Always a good beginning," she murmured as his hands

brushed her shoulder blades.

"A prince who found a princess working in a bar." He held the ties to her dress, one in each hand. If he let go, the front would drop to her waist.

"Do all of your stories involve bartenders?" she teased, interrupting the mental picture of her bare breasts.

"Yes. When it comes to the 'good parts' in my stories, I have a one-track mind." He leaned forward and brushed his lips over her shoulder. "I need you to turn around before I continue."

She shifted and he released the fabric, watching as it slipped over her skin and revealed her chest. He stared, trying like hell to draft an impromptu fairytale in his head when all he wanted to do was fall to his knees and worship her tits. He was pretty damn sure he could make her feel like royalty with his tongue instead of his words.

"Go on," she said, raising her hands to her breasts.

"The prince knew he'd lose his fucking mind if he ever got this woman alone," he said, his gaze fixed on her hands as he reached for the loose dress clinging to her hips. "The thought of her naked…"

One tug and the gray material pooled at her feet. She still wore the shoes they'd purchased during her shopping dare, but nothing else. Jack lowered one knee to the ground and reached for the zipper on her right foot.

The temptation to run his lips over her legs, licking his way up her thighs—he focused on her feet as if he cared about her shoes. He quickly released the second zipper and stood up. If he stayed down there too long, he would bury his face between her legs and taste her. End of story.

"The thought of her naked left him speechless?" she asked, kicking off her shoes.

"Yeah."

She lifted her breasts and pushed them together. Her

thumbs teased her nipples. And he had to touch her. Placing his hands on her hips, he drew her close.

He growled and fought to find the words. "It blew his mind. He wanted to lift her up, carry her to bed, and toss her onto the petals."

"Oh, God…"

His mouth formed a thin line. She needed more. He knew she wasn't ready until she added "Jack" to her heavenly pleas.

"But he wanted to make love to the princess on her terms. He wanted to earn her trust."

"He has it," she said softly. "The princess—she was hiding behind fear. But not anymore."

He fought the temptation to toss her over his shoulder, follow the roses straight to the bed, and prove she meant what she said. But he wasn't here to test her.

"You're interrupting," he said.

"Sorry. Please continue."

"The prince offered her three wishes." He ran his hands over her ass and rocked his hips. "Wish number one…"

He lifted his gaze to her face and raised an eyebrow. This was her call.

She released her breasts, placed her hand on his chest, and gave him a light push. "I wish Prince Charming would sit down on the rose petals and tell me more."

He backed away from her, careful to avoid the romantic flower obstacle course on the carpet. The back of his calves touched the bedframe and he sat. "Tonight, he wanted the princess to pick the position," he said. "Did she want to be on top of him, grinding against him? Or pinned to the bed beneath—"

"On top," she said as she approached the bed. She placed one knee on either side of his hips, rested her hands on his shoulders, and sank into his lap. She was wet and hot and ready. "To start," she added.

He groaned as his hand ran over her back and down to her ass. "Darlin' tell me what you need from me. I'll do whatever I can to make it happen. But I'm not sure how much longer I'll be able to string together coherent sentences."

She rocked her hips against him.

"Natalie," he growled. He wanted to come inside her, not pressing up against her like this.

"May I use my second wish?" she asked.

"*Anything.*"

"I wish for a condom."

"You don't need to waste a wish on that." He turned his head and scanned the sheets. He'd seen a few tossed among the rose petals as if Natalie had been thinking ahead to this moment. "Protection is included along with your favorite sexual position."

He located the shiny, square packet that looked nothing like a rose petal, and grabbed it off the sheets. She took it from him and tore it open. She reached between them and quickly covered him.

"Jack?" She raised her hips but stopped short of sinking down and burying his dick inside her.

"Yeah?" he gasped. If she demanded another chapter to the story—shit, he wasn't sure he could deliver. He was about five seconds away from a serious reduction in his vocabulary. "Please" and "Natalie" would be the extent of his storytelling skills.

"I've never felt like a princess—I've never felt this happy," she said, her brown eyes staring into his. "Until now. I want to thank you. For all of it."

"There's no fucking way I'm getting a pen and paper for you right now," he said.

"I don't need one." She wrapped one hand around the base of his cock and guided him in.

His hands pressed into the mattress and his hips lifted to

greet her. "Shit, I'm sorry," he muttered. "I couldn't resist. But now it's your turn. Set the pace. Ride me, grind against me — whatever you need, take it. Take me."

"Hmm," she murmured as she rocked her hips against him and closed her eyes. She arched her back, pressing her breasts up toward his mouth. "I have one more wish, Prince Charming."

"Done," he growled.

"Don't hold back," she ordered.

"Natalie." He placed a hand on her lower back. The need to touch her overrode his plans. Her words pushed him over the edge. One second he was under control. And the next thing he knew, he had his hands wrapped around her waist. He lifted her up. And his body moved with her, holding her close, maintaining their intimate connection. Until he turned to the bed and lifted her off his dick and laid her down on the bed.

"Jack," she protested.

"I'm not holding back," he said, covering her body with his and thrusting inside her. They could get creative later. Right now, he needed her beneath him. "Wrap your legs around me and hold on, darlin'. I'm going to blow your mind."

Three hard thrusts, her hips rising to meet his, and she screamed the words he'd been waiting to hear from the moment he'd knocked on her door.

"Oh God, Jack!"

She arched and writhed beneath him. And shit, the things she was doing to his dick…

It took all his self-control and then some to hold back. Because he wasn't ready to follow her over the cliff. Not just yet.

"Jack?" she whispered as her movements slowed beneath him.

He straightened his arms, allowing his hands to support

his upper body as he looked down at her. On the heels of her orgasm, he saw a rainbow of emotions flicker across her face. Fear. Wonder. Surprise. And something that looked a helluva lot like a teenage girl meeting her favorite boy band member.

"Are you okay?" he asked. The fear, the wonder, and even the surprise, he understood those feelings. But the You're-My-Hero look? No one had ever gazed at him quite like that.

"I'm falling in love with the sound of your voice," she admitted. "And with you."

I'm falling in love.

That look—it wasn't hero worship, or a full-blown crush. It was love.

And dammit, he was still inside of her, his dick primed to explode in five, four, three, two—

"Darlin', I can't…" He closed his eyes. *Love.* Natalie was falling in love with him. "Fuck."

Maybe he just couldn't hold on any longer, buried inside her. Or maybe the fact that she'd said the magic word that spelled out how he felt about her pushed him over the edge. Either way, the orgasm rocked through him.

"Natalie," he roared. "Natalie!"

I'm *falling in love with you.*

Natalie watched as every muscle in his body tightened as he came—*in response to her words.*

And okay, he was buried inside of her. It wasn't like she'd sat down across the coffee table in the sitting area, said the l-word, and he'd come in his pants. She couldn't take this as a sign that he'd fallen too. She needed to hear him say the words.

She felt his body relax. And then slowly, gently, he rolled off of her.

"So I guess this means you never want me to shut up?" He turned on his side and supported his head with his hand, his elbow pushing into the mattress. "Stupid pick-up lines, bedtime stories—you want me to keep talking?"

"Yes, Jack. I want you to talk to me. And I promise to listen. Just make sure you're picking *me* up with your lines."

"I will." He placed his hand on her heart. "Because I started falling in love with you the moment I walked into your bar. I've been falling ever since. I love you, Natalie. I love that you hear me, that you understand how the past messed me up."

"It did a number on me too," she murmured.

"And those fears don't just walk out of your life because you want them to," he said. "But even when you're scared, even when all the shit you've lived through comes back to haunt you, I'm still going to love you."

"Jack," she murmured, covering his hand with hers.

When was the last time someone had walked into her life and looked past her failings? Her foster families had handed her off, making her someone else's problem. Her best friend, and until recently, even Lucia, had given her the space she demanded. But not Jack. He'd grabbed a rope and tried to climb her walls and peek over the edge. He wanted to see her fears—to see *her*.

And yes, that had terrified her at first and sent her running, unable to trust in him. But no one outside of her family—and Cade—had offered to love her just as she was. Just the opposite. They'd turned her away. And even those closest to her, including her sister and her best friend, had loved her from a distance. But Jack was right here, his hand on her heart, his naked body lying beside her, loving her, understanding her.

It was almost too much. His love was like this great big gift. What could she possibly offer him in return? Her heart?

It didn't feel like enough for the man who'd given her a second chance, allowing her to work through her fears.

"I think it's time for the black silk ties," she said. His fantasy, his desires—she could give him that.

He shook his head. "Not tonight. We'll get there. Don't get me wrong. I love the fact that you went out and bought those. I look forward to using your present. But there's no rush. I'll settle for reverse cowgirl and maybe one of your special blow jobs."

She stared up at him as relief rushed through her. He'd accepted her gift for exactly what it was—a sign that she wanted to carry their fantasy world forward into the future, into a relationship, and into reality. But he wasn't pushing her. There was always tomorrow and the day after that.

She slid off the bed, walked over to the armchair, and picked up the lengths of black silk. Then she turned and headed for the man she'd fallen in love with. He'd sat up. His long legs were stretched out in front of him on the bed. His palms pressed into the sheets, supporting his upper body as he leaned back, the pose putting his muscles on display.

She stopped at the edge of the bed and tossed her present onto his lap. "I don't want to wait. You're deploying soon. This could be our last chance to make your fantasy come true."

"Natalie, the silk ties aren't the fantasy." He picked them up and set the ties aside as he moved to the edge of the bed. He sat with his feet planted on the floor. He reached forward and grabbed ahold of her hands. "You are."

"Jack, from the beginning you've talked about tying me up."

"Because I wanted to turn you on. Because I wanted you," he said firmly. "Natalie, you're the fantasy. I'm not here, asking for a chance to be a part of your life, to love you and be loved in return because I'm looking for kinky sex. If that is what you want, and you trust me enough to enjoy it, then hell yeah, I'm in. But if you just want to hear that story over and over while those ties gather dust bunnies under the bed, that works for me, too."

She pulled his hands and stepped back. He stood and allowed her to press her body up against his. Closing her eyes, still holding his hands, she rested her head against his chest.

"What if you don't come back?" she whispered. "What if your fantasy collects dust bunnies because you never returned to claim it?"

He released her hands and his arms banded around her. She felt one hand running down her back, a gentle, reassuring caress. She wanted to believe in him, in their future.

"You can be scared," he said. "But I don't think that's how our story ends, Natalie. I'm not leaving behind the woman I love without a fight. And you know, I'm looking forward to the day when you say, 'Tie me up in the back room of the bar, Jack.' That's a pretty damn good incentive to stay alive."

Even the best training wouldn't guarantee protection against an IED. And she knew the bad guys carried powerful weapons. What if he was sent into an ISIS stronghold to rescue a hostage?

She lived with these fears every time Cade deployed. But thinking about Jack out there? Not knowing if he'd have a tomorrow?

Except he lived with that same fear but faced it every time he went on a mission. She'd honor him, then, and lift him up with her love. Let him fight for what mattered and know that he had the strength of her love waiting for him back home.

"I dare you to come back." She wrapped her arms around him, holding tight to her charming SEAL. "Because one day, I'm going to dare you to use those black silk ties. And so much more, Jack. So much more."

Epilogue

Dear Natalie,

I might not have a chance to write over the next couple of days. I can't say more than that, but I promise to stay safe. Cade, Dante, Ronan, and the rest of the team have my back. I'm coming home to you, darlin'. And we're taking that vacation you keep talking about and going down to Texas. I want you to meet my mom. And yeah, I'm looking forward to watching you take on Colton again.

But until I'm back, I wanted to leave you with another story to read late at night when you're alone. And shit, the thought of you in your bed, your fingers between your legs... I'm hard right now just thinking about you.

So here it goes, fantasy number—hell, I forget. Twenty? Thirty? I can't remember how many I've mailed out since I left Coronado. But you can thank me when I get back. No pen and paper needed.

How to Fuck a Princess: Part Twenty or Maybe Thirty in a Never-ending Series

Once upon a time, at the end of a long bartending shift, the princess locked up and headed for her car. As she walked through the parking lot, she could feel someone watching her. She moved to the trunk of her car, unlocked it, and reached inside.

Her silent spectator abandoned the shadows. She recognized him. She'd been waiting for this man.

"Spread your legs," he ordered. "And keep your hands on the floor of the trunk."

She obeyed. And he moved behind her, reaching for the hem of her short, tight skirt. (You do own one of those, don't you darlin'?)

"Don't move," he said as he stepped back to admire the view under the full moon. He'd looked up at that moon, thinking about her and dreaming about this moment for so long. Now, her white thong caught the light, begging to be pulled down her perfect legs.

And while he was down there, he would steal a taste—

"Jack?"

He looked up from the legal pad as Ronan walked into the team's makeshift base. Dante followed at his heels, heading straight for Jack's folding table.

Jack carefully rested his forearms over his words.

"What the hell man?" Ronan demanded. "Working on your novel again?"

"A letter to Natalie," he said. As his teammates damn well knew. He wrote to her every chance he got, sometimes two or three letters at a time to cover the days he couldn't sit down with a pen and paper.

"You know," Dante said. "There's this thing called email. Saves the cost of postage and she can read it right away on her phone."

But she couldn't hold it in her hands. Not that she needed a physical letter to get off—which he hoped like hell she did once in a while, picturing the scenes he'd spelled out. But a letter offered tangible proof that he was still alive and fantasizing about her.

"You're going to have to finish another time," Ronan said, his tone packing an overdose of grim. "We just received a go order. Time to get those hostages out of there and take them home."

Natalie stood behind the bar and sifted through the mail. In a few minutes, she'd unlock the front door and start her shift. But first, she had to find it, the envelope from someplace far, far away. Somewhere, buried between the bills and junk mail, was another letter. One arrived almost every day. Some days, she got two.

Her phone vibrated beside the pile of useless mail. She picked it up and scanned the name on the screen.

Prince Charming.

"Jack?" she said, answering the call and pressing the phone to her ear.

"Hi, Natalie."

Her knees gave out and she sank to the floor behind her bar, blocking out everything but the sound of his voice.

"Jack, where are you?" Stupid question. He couldn't answer that. And she might lose their connection any second. "Are you okay?"

"I'm fine," he said. "And I'm home. In fact, I'm—"

"Home? In Coronado?" she demanded, pushing herself off the barroom floor.

"I'm right outside your door."

She heard a knock on the locked door to the bar. Tossing her phone aside, she rushed to open it.

"Jack," she cried, flinging herself into his arms. She held tight, pressing her body up against him, unwilling to pull back far enough to kiss him. Right now, she just needed to hear his heart beating in his chest.

"You did it," she whispered against his T-shirt. "You stayed alive."

And he'd come back to her. He'd kept his promise.

"We did a helluva lot better than that," he said, running one hand through her hair while the other pressed against her back as if he needed to keep her close. "We pulled out three American hostages. Aid workers kidnapped in Iraq."

"Wait." She looked up at him. "You're not allowed to tell me."

"You'll hear about it on the news tonight." He lowered his lips to hers and stole a quick kiss. "Maybe tomorrow. They won't identify my team by name. But the reports will mention SEALs. They'll probably talk about how one of the team—Dante—got hurt during the rescue. He'll be all right. Just sidelined while he heals."

And just like that it was over. He was here, in her arms. Three hostages had a chance at a future because of him. And Jack was here. In her bar…

"Don't move," she ordered, pulling free from his arms.

He laughed. "I'm not going anywhere."

He followed her to the bar, waiting on the customers' side as she slipped behind it and retrieved her bag. She opened it and riffled through the file folder she carried with her everywhere until she found the piece of paper she was looking for. She scanned the words, confirming that this was the correct fantasy.

Black silk ties…the stainless steel table…her arms bound…

She stood, reached across the bar, and handed him the very first letter he'd sent her—a written account of their first bedtime story from the motel on the way to her sister's wedding.

"I'm ready, Jack. Take me into the back room and tie me up."

"Natalie," he said as heat and desire eclipsed all other emotions in his blue eyes.

"Take me. I'm ready. I trust you. Completely, I swear. With my body and with my heart, I trust you." She took a step back toward the swinging door to the back room. But she kept her gaze locked with his. "The silk ties I bought in Vegas? They're waiting for us."

She took another step back and then another.

He glanced down at the letter in his hand. "You keep this with you?"

"I carry your fantasies with me everywhere I go." Her back pressed up against the door. "And now, I'm ready to make this one a reality."

"You're sure?"

"Yes. Now, come with me, Prince Charming." She offered him her best hand-over-your-boxers smile. "I dare you."

Acknowledgments

First, I owe my readers a huge thank you and probably a Facebook party. And at this party, everyone leaves with a prize! (You are all following me on Facebook right? It's my favorite place to chat with readers.) I've dreamed about writing a Navy SEAL series for years. Thank you for making the publication of this series a dream come true!

Second, thank you to my wonderful agent, Jill Marsal for her endless support and brilliant feedback. I also owe the entire Entangled team, including my editor Heather Howland, a debt of gratitude. I know you work tirelessly behind the scenes to make each book a success. Thank you for everything you do!

I wrote Jack and Natalie's story in long bursts of creative energy. And it was so much fun! While I was writing, my supportive husband took the kids. He allowed me to write for twenty-four hours straight (or more sometimes!) Thank you my love!

About the Author

Sara Jane Stone lives in Brooklyn, New York, with her very supportive real-life hero, two lively young children, and a lazy Burmese cat. When she is not finger painting with the kids, she loves writing sexy stories, staying up past her bedtime reading red-hot romance, and chatting with her readers on Facebook.

Discover the **Sin City SEALs** *series...*

To Tempt a SEAL

For the first time in her life, art therapist Lucia Lewis is ready to live. And the masquerade ball in Las Vegas is just the place to find a ridiculously hot guy to complete her wicked to-do list. The only rule? That the mask concealing her scars stays *on*. Navy SEAL Cade Daniels is on a mission to keep his best friend's little sister out of trouble, but instead, he finds complete and absolute temptation. And it could cost him the one thing he isn't willing to risk...his heart.